The fire snapped and sizzled then quieted, and for what seemed like an eternity, silence yawned in the darkness between them. Knowing that he didn't have all the answers made him seem a bit less powerful, which in turn made her feel a bit less helpless.

Without deliberate intent, she began to relax. She also began to feel sleepy, but then suddenly it seemed important that she tell him something.

"Brice?" she whispered, rushing on before he could answer. "I didn't mean to hurt Rowena. It was so dark that night. I honestly didn't see her. If I could take back what happened, I'd do it in a minute. In a minute. You have no idea—" Her voice cracked. She stopped. When Brice said nothing, she turned over, closed her eyes and prayed that he'd believe her.

For some reason, that mattered to her very much.

"Barbara Delinsky knows the human heart and its immense capacity to love and to believe."
—*Washington* (PA) *Observer-Reporter*

Also available from MIRA Books and
BARBARA DELINSKY

THROUGH MY EYES
CARDINAL RULES
MONTANA MAN
THE DREAM
THE DREAM UNFOLDS
THE DREAM COMES TRUE
HAVING FAITH
THE OUTSIDER
THE REAL THING
CHANCES ARE
THE STUD
DREAMS
TWELVE ACROSS

Coming soon

FIRST, BEST AND ONLY
September 2001

BARBARA
DELINSKY
T.L.C.

MIRA®

If you purchased this book without a cover you should be aware
that this book is stolen property. It was reported as "unsold and
destroyed" to the publisher, and neither the author nor the
publisher has received any payment for this "stripped book."

ISBN 1-55166-822-X

T.L.C.

Copyright © 1987 by Barbara Delinsky.

All rights reserved. Except for use in any review, the reproduction or
utilization of this work in whole or in part in any form by any electronic,
mechanical or other means, now known or hereafter invented, including
xerography, photocopying and recording, or in any information storage or
retrieval system, is forbidden without the written permission of the publisher,
MIRA Books, 225 Duncan Mill Road, Don Mills, Ontario, Canada M3B 3K9.

All characters in this book have no existence outside the imagination of the
author and have no relation whatsoever to anyone bearing the same name
or names. They are not even distantly inspired by any individual known or
unknown to the author, and all incidents are pure invention.

MIRA and the Star Colophon are trademarks used under license and registered
in Australia, New Zealand, Philippines, United States Patent and Trademark
Office and in other countries.

Visit us at www.mirabooks.com

Printed in U.S.A.

T.L.C.

1

Under normal circumstances, Karen Drew would have found the article intriguing. She was a devoted armchair traveler—the more exotic the locale the better—and the tropical Seychelles, with their gentle breezes and sun-tipped turquoise seas, sounded perfectly idyllic compared to upstate New York in February.

Today, though, visions of coco-de-mer palms, giant tortoises and white sand beaches just weren't doing it for her. Her energies were concentrated on seeing the words on the magazine page, speaking them aloud in a relatively normal manner and, in the process, breathing as little as possible on Rowena Carlin.

Karen was sick. She'd been fighting a cold for nearly three weeks. It had flared up, died down, looked to be going away, only to rear its stubborn head in renewed bouts of sniffling and coughing. Now it had settled in her chest. No battery of antihistamines, decongestants or expectorants was budging it. Though Karen had fortified herself enough to temporarily mask the symptoms, each breath she took was an effort.

She couldn't afford to be sick. Thought of it sent her into a tailspin. Midterms were coming. Even without those, she had research to do for Professor McGuire and, even beyond that, tables to wait at the Pepper Mill. Paychecks weren't given for nothing, and Karen needed the money. So she'd spent the last three weeks ignoring the germ that plagued her. Unfortunately, it wasn't going away. It had slowly but surely sapped her, leaving her fighting for the tiniest shreds of energy.

On the tail of one such shred, she shifted the glossy magazine from which she'd been reading onto the plaid blanket that covered the older woman's small lap. "See, Rowena?" she asked. "Isn't it beautiful?"

Rowena, who had been raptly studying Karen's face, lowered her eyes to look at the magazine, but no sooner did they reach their destination than they started right back up again. The look they held made Karen brace herself. If she'd learned one thing in the eight months she'd been visiting Rowena, it was that the woman missed very little and let even less pass without comment.

Rowena was eighty-one and sharp. A spinal injury had hindered her mobility, a subsequent stroke had affected her speech. Nothing, though, had affected her mind—or her eyes, which said far more far faster than her tongue could. Those eyes held concern even as the small, wizened mouth went to work.

"S-s-something is…wrong," she announced. Her speech was faltering, yet far better than it had been even three months before. Karen was amazed at her improvement—both in speech and movement. Rowena approached physical therapy with a will to succeed, and she was doing just that. The fact that her arms and legs were slowly coming back to life was a tribute to sheer determination. Karen followed her example and answered as confidently as she could.

"No, no. Nothing's wrong."

"Y-y-you're under the...w-w-weather."

Karen crinkled her nose and gave a quick shake of her head, which was a mistake. When her head turned right, her awareness stayed left, and when her head turned left, she felt as though she'd bumped into herself at the pass. The air in the small parlor seemed suddenly warmer.

It was a minute before she regained her equilibrium and a minute after that before she quelled the urge to cough. When she spoke, her voice was husky. "I'm just a little tired. It's a busy time. Midterms begin in two weeks." She paused when she saw Rowena's mouth working again. Patiently she waited, giving the woman the time she needed to form the words.

"Will y-y-you have a rest...then?"

If only, Karen thought. "A little," she said. "I'll have two weeks without classes, so it'll just be a matter of working."

"F-f-for...McGuire?"

"Uh-huh."

"And the...r-r-restaurant?"

"That's right."

"Karen?"

"Uh-huh?"

"Take a...v-v-vacation."

Karen's eyes held a wistful look. "I wish I could."

"Y-y-you…can if…you…want."

"No. My hours at the restaurant will be shortened since most of the customers will be gone, but I'm committed to working full-time for Professor McGuire during those weeks."

"And visiting me. It's…t-t-too much."

"But I *enjoy* visiting you."

"D-d-do you enjoy…y-y-your work, too?"

Karen desperately wanted to say that she did, but she couldn't do so unequivocally. While she found her work for Professor McGuire to be intellectually rewarding, the only reward she gleaned from her work at the Pepper Mill was a pocketful of tips. The restaurant was heavily patronized by students, and deep down, she had trouble dealing with them. Some were in her classes; others she knew only in passing. Theoretically, she might have shared in the camaraderie.

But she didn't. For one thing, there was the age difference. At twenty-nine, she was a good ten years older than many of them. For another, there was the socioeconomic difference. These were wealthy kids. They weren't working two jobs on top of classes, as she was. They weren't living on shoestring budgets in small rooms off campus, either; they were well enough off to pass up the dining hall food their parents paid for in favor of regular meals at the Pepper Mill.

In small groups they were fine—inoffensive, even congenial. Often, though, groups of five, six or more came in, and at those times, Karen wished them on any other waitress but herself. Large groups tended to be boisterous and demanding, sometimes even obnoxious.

But that was the downside. Looking to the upside, she said, "My work isn't all that bad. Professor McGuire has me researching the lives of obscure artists, several of whom, I'm sure, won't be obscure too much longer—" she pressed her lips tightly together to ward off a sneeze, and when it had passed, went on "—and the Pepper Mill makes super nachos."

"Y-y-you eat there?"

"Dinner every night that I work." Which was five days a week.

"Do they…make you…p-p-pay?"

"No. The owners are generous about that."

Rowena's concern just then wasn't with the owners. "Nachos…aren't…n-n-nourishing."

"Maybe not, but they sure taste good."

"Too…thin."

Karen knew Rowena wasn't referring to the nachos. "Me? Nah. Thin is in." Her n's were growing more dense, which meant that the nasal spray she'd used before she'd left home had begun to wear off, which meant she had just a few minutes left before she'd be stopped up.

"T-t-too…thin," Rowena repeated firmly.

Not up to arguing, Karen retrieved the magazine and read on for several more minutes, but her eyes grew progressively heavy and her cheeks progressively hot. She found the room increasingly stuffy in spite of the chill that seeped from the window behind her. Her voice sounded tighter, her chest felt tighter, and her body had begun to ache in spots it hadn't ached before. The aspirin was wearing off, too, she realized. She felt horrid.

Gently closing the magazine, she sent Rowena an apologetic glance. "I think," she said tentatively, "that I ought to head home. I'm working tonight."

Rowena's gaze slid from Karen's face to the window. Something in her look made Karen turn.

Not only had it begun to snow, but it was snowing hard. "Oh dear," she murmured under her breath. Home was in Syracuse, which was a forty-five-minute drive from the nursing home under normal conditions. Over snowy roads it was bound to take longer. If she were feeling fine, that wouldn't be much of a problem. But she wasn't feeling fine. She wasn't looking forward to stepping foot outside the nursing home, let alone tackling the storm in her aging Chevy.

But it had to be done. "I'll be okay," she said, brows knitting as she tucked the magazine into her shoulder pouch. Taking a slow breath for strength, she stood, then reached for the coat she'd dropped on a nearby chair when she'd arrived.

A momentary wave of dizziness hit her. Bracing her legs against the side of the chair in which she'd been sitting, she took several shallow breaths and willed the dizziness away. Mercifully, it went.

"Driving...c-c-could be bad," Rowena warned.

Karen felt a chill even through the wool of her topcoat. Fingers slightly unsteady, she worked the last two buttons through their holes and tried to sound philosophical. "Actually, I've been impressed. People up here take the snow in stride. The highway crews are pretty good about keeping the roads plowed and sanded.'' She wrapped a long wool scarf around her neck once, then a second time. ''Besides, it's been a snowy winter, which makes me a veteran. I'd probably be more nervous if I were back in New York.''

''Do you...m-m-miss it?''

''The city?'' She stuffed one hand into a mitten and curled her fingers around the wool in a blind search for warmth. ''Not really. It was—is—so hectic.''

''Your life here is...hectic.''

Pulling on her second mitten, Karen shot Rowena a gently chiding glance. ''You're not supposed to know that. You're supposed to think I'm a woman of leisure.''

Rowena's eyes made mockery of the idea. ''Y-y-you wouldn't...ever be a...w-w-woman of leisure.''

Karen didn't have to ask how she knew. She and Rowena were kindred souls—both curious, both strong-willed, both dreamers. From the start they'd hit it off. Karen would easily bet that Rowena had never in her life been a woman of leisure. And neither had she.

''Do you mean to say,'' she ventured in as playful a tone as she could muster, ''that I don't look totally laid back—calm, cool and collected?'' When Rowena simply pursed her lips, Karen made a tiny face. ''I look frazzled?''

''Sick.''

She supposed sick was better than frazzled and perhaps more correct at the moment. "I'm tired."

"Go...home."

Aware that her head was beginning to throb, Karen hoisted her bag to her shoulder. "If I didn't know better," she managed to tease hoarsely, "I'd think you were trying to get rid of me." She held up a mittened hand. "I'm going. I'm going." Then she dropped all pretense of teasing. She hated leaving Rowena. The woman gave her a kind of comfort that she couldn't quite explain. "I'll see you Tuesday, okay?"

"Only if...y-y-you're...f-f-feeling better."

"I'll be fine."

"D-d-drive slowly."

"I don't think I'll have a choice today."

Rowena's eyes, riveted to Karen's face, grew more worried. "Maybe...you should...s-s-stay here."

All the nursing home needed, Karen mused, was a bundle of germs in its midst. She felt badly enough being near Rowena, but she couldn't have not come. Twice weekly she visited. Those visits had become as vital a part of her schedule as anything else she did.

"No, Rowena," she said gently. "I have to drive home."

"Then...w-w-wait awhile."

Casting a glance out the window, Karen considered that, only to reluctantly veto the idea. "The longer I wait, the worse the driving may be. They're expecting me at the restaurant later, and when I'm done there,

I have a history paper to start. I was planning to spend most of tomorrow finishing it.''

"Tomorrow is…S-S-Saturday. N-n-no date?''

"Nope,'' Karen said with deliberate nonchalance. "I'm working the late shift.''

"You don't usually.''

"I know, but Saturday nights are busy, which means good money. And since things will be quieting down really soon…'' She let her words trail off, realizing that it was taking more and more of an effort to force them out. "Gotta run, Rowena. Really.'' She bent forward to tug the blanket a little higher on Rowena's lap. "You take care now. Anything special I can bring on Tuesday?''

She always asked, she was always refused—as she was now with a look. Rowena Carlin was an independent soul, but Karen could appreciate that, too.

"Take…c-c-care of *your*self,'' Rowena advised.

"Will do,'' Karen said. She gave the older woman's shoulder a gentle touch before starting for the door. There she stopped for a final, fond glance back. "See you Tuesday,'' she promised and forced herself on.

Once clear of the parlor arch and Rowena's all-seeing gaze, she paused, lowered her head and closed her eyes for an instant, then took a stuffy breath and went on. When she reached the desk just inside the front door, she paused again, this time to speak softly to the receptionist.

"Judy, I've just left Mrs. Carlin. Will you see that someone gets her?''

Judy smiled. She was a young girl, a high school junior who spent her afternoons at the nursing home. She knew Rowena nearly as well as Karen did and understood that the elderly woman wouldn't have stood for being ''gotten'' in Karen's presence.

''Sure thing, Ms Drew.''

Karen nodded her thanks as she turned to look through the window at the fast-falling snow. She couldn't contain a husky moan.

Judy was in instant sympathy. ''I only live two blocks from here. You've driven a ways. I'm surprised you did it today. They've been talking about snow since last night.''

''I didn't know.''

''What do you listen to?''

''What what?''

''Radio station. In the car?''

''I don't.''

Judy stared at her in genuine disbelief. ''Don't you get bored? I'd go out of my mind without music, especially driving the distance you do.''

''Unfortunately,'' Karen said with a weak sigh, ''I don't have a radio—well, I have one but it hasn't worked since I bought the car, and I couldn't see spending the money to fix it when there were so many more critical repairs to be done.''

''Sounds like you bought a clunker.''

''No. It's just seen better days.''

Judy's young face lit up. ''Want my brother to take a look at it? He's great with cars.''

''I'll remember that if I run into trouble,'' Karen

said, casting another worried glance at the snow. "Which may be very soon."

Judy followed Karen's glance. "Are you sure you want to go out in that?"

Karen started to sigh but broke into a low, thick cough. She covered her mouth, turned her head, controlled the cough, then said, "I don't have much choice."

"You could stick around for a while, see if it lets up, y'know?"

"Is that what the forecast says it's going to do?"

"No."

"How much are we in for?"

"Eight to twelve inches."

Bowing her head, Karen pressed wool-sheathed fingertips to the aching spot between her eyes. Actually, she was aching all over. Her fingers felt like ice inside the mittens. At the same time, her nose was beaded with sweat. The sooner she got home, the better.

Tightening the scarf around her neck, she tucked her shoulder bag firmly beneath her arm, gave Judy a quick wave, and forced herself out the door.

She was hit in the face by the snow. Hard little nuggets of cold stuff, tiny ice pellets driven by the wind felt like needles against her hot cheeks. Ducking her head and slitting her eyes, she focused on her feet. She took one step, a second, a third in rapid and steady succession. Her boots sank into no more than an inch of snow, yet she felt she was trudging through a foot. The fourth step required more of an effort than the third had, the fifth more than the fourth.

She plugged on. Tucking her head even lower against the frigid gusts, she hastened her step. At least she thought that was what she was doing, but the walk seemed endless. She put a shoulder to the wind and led with it, at the same time glancing back at the nursing home. It seemed far away, separated from her by a wall of sheeting snow.

Finally reaching the end of the walk, she skidded onto the driveway and half slid, half trotted to her car. Snow had started to mount on the windshield, but the wind had prevented it from doing so elsewhere. She batted a mittened hand across the slight accumulation, then tugged off the mitten, reached in her pocket for the key, opened the door and threw herself inside. The slam of the door beside her was accompanied by a heavy cough. She sat still for a minute, breathing shallowly, with her head against the headrest and her eyes closed.

But that wasn't going to get her home, and home was where she wanted to be. So though her head felt like a brick, she raised it and turned the key in the ignition.

Nothing happened.

Shoving the scarf away from her face, she tried again. Still nothing happened. The motor didn't even turn over.

This time when she closed her eyes, she bowed her head to the steering wheel and moaned. It was the battery. She knew it was. For weeks now, the car had been giving her little messages, hinting that something inside it was getting tired and worn. She hadn't listened because she'd felt tired and worn herself. She hadn't had energy to spend on the car, much less time or money.

That had been short-sighted of her.

Raising her head, she forced herself to think clearly. Her eyes felt dry and hot, but she trained them on the gearshift. She was in park. The car should start. Hands shaking, she removed the key from the ignition, checked to see that she had the right one, reinserted it, turned it.

She stepped on the gas pedal once, slowly, then turned the key again. She stepped on the gas a second time, then a third and a fourth while she flicked the ignition switch from off to on, back and forth with a breath in between.

She reached for the broken radio to make sure it was off. She turned off the heat. She checked to make sure the windshield wipers were off. She turned the key again.

Shivering now from the cold, she peered at the fuel gauge and felt a wave of relief. The needle was on empty. She was out of gas. Then it occurred to her that the needle was always on empty when the engine was off. And she'd filled the car three days before.

Swallowing painfully, she cast a helpless gaze skyward. A dead battery in the middle of a snowstorm. Swell.

Simply because she didn't have the strength to move, she sat where she was for the course of a minute, which was long enough for her to realize that if she remained much longer, she'd freeze. Snow was pelting the windshield. The swathe she'd brushed clear had been covered again. Even worse, gusts of wind rocked the car, sending the chill to her bones.

Having no recourse, she tucked the keys back in her pocket, put her mitten on and climbed from the car. The force of the wind made her stagger for an instant. She pulled the scarf higher to cover her hair, but the wind quickly blew it back down, so she ducked her head as she'd done before and set out over her own fast-fading footprints.

She didn't get far before another wave of dizziness hit. This time she didn't have a chair to rest against, so she stood swaying in the storm, taking shallow breaths, which was all her congested lungs would allow. She was hot on the inside, cold on the outside. Her knees felt rubbery, and she wanted nothing more than to lie down for just a few minutes. She'd do that while she waited for someone to jump start her car. Just a few minute's rest and she'd be fine.

The problem was getting back to the nursing home. Her legs didn't seem to want to work, and the dizziness wasn't going away. Her body wasn't cooperating, she realized in dismay. But she had to get inside. She had to do it quickly. The world was growing whiter and whiter. She'd never feared the snow, but there was something strange about it now. It was growing too thick, becoming a wooly blanket that could either freeze or suffocate her. And the noise…she hadn't thought snow made that kind of buzzing sound.…

* * *

Brice Carlin had pulled into a parking space just as Karen was leaving the nursing home. Turning off his engine, he watched her fight her way through the storm to the car beside his. Still comfortable in the slow-ebbing heat, he sat for a minute longer. When she remained motionless, he wondered why she didn't start her car. When she dropped her forehead to the wheel, he felt perverse satisfaction.

So she felt bad? Good. She *should* feel bad.

But rather than leaving his car and showing his disdain by stalking past her into the nursing home, he continued to watch. He couldn't understand what she was doing, why she didn't start her car if for no other reason than to turn on the heat. It was freezing. The windchill factor had tumbled the temperature to zero. Yet she simply sat there, leaning slightly forward, seemingly preoccupied with the dashboard.

At last she settled back in the seat, inert for the space of a minute. Through the snow-studded glass, Brice could make out most of her profile, and what he couldn't make out he remembered. He remembered well. For two days he'd studied her with neither car windows nor snow to fog his view. He remembered well the wide eyes, the straight nose, the gentle lips. He remembered well her look of innocence, which had annoyed him, and of worry, which had given him a measure of comfort. That comfort had disappeared on the day she'd been acquitted.

Jaw tighter than it had been moments before, he saw her move. He waited to hear the rev of her engine, but instead she climbed from the car and started

back toward the home. He assumed she'd forgotten
something and glanced at the digital display on his
dashboard. It was nearly four o'clock. He didn't want
to sit there forever. Then again, if he left the car and
went inside, he'd risk a head-on confrontation, and he
wasn't sure he trusted himself for that. So he sat and
monitored her progress.

It slowed, then came to a halt.

He was beginning to think that she was screwy on
top of everything else when she swayed. She seemed
about to fall, then caught herself, and he assumed
she'd been taken off guard by the wind. Then she
swayed again. She was halfway to the ground when
it suddenly hit him that she wasn't well.

Without another thought, he threw open his door
and bolted from the car. Karen was in a limp heap,
dead to the world when he reached her. Scooping her
into his arms, he lifted her from the snow and started
toward the nursing home only to stop and press his
lips together, then do an about-face. Moments later
he was depositing her into the passenger seat of his
car, where he took a minute to examine her. Her forehead and cheeks were hot to the touch. Her skin had
an unearthly pallor. Her breathing was quick, shallow
and labored.

Having seen enough, he closed the door, rounded
the car to the driver's side, slid behind the wheel and
took off.

Very slowly, Karen returned to awareness. She felt
cold and hot and achy. She also felt light, as though
she'd been floating and had just touched down. Only

she was still moving. Or something was moving under her. It came to her gradually that she was going to have to open her eyes.

The first thing she saw when she did so was a dashboard with a strange display of buttons, gauges, dials and readouts. She felt more disoriented than ever. Needing a familiar point of reference, she raised her gaze to the windshield. Snow was hitting it—that rang a familiar bell—but the wipers were working, and hers hadn't been. Her car hadn't been working, period. This one was. And even if it had been her car, she wasn't driving.

Blinking once, then again, she tipped her head just the slightest bit and looked at the driver. That was when stark fear hit.

His profile was unfamiliar and totally intimidating. His hair was dark, his features chiseled and tight. The collar of his topcoat stood up against his nape and was as dark as the insides of the car.

With a strength born of panic, she grabbed the handle of the door and tugged it. She would have tumbled out had not an arm snagged her middle and hauled her back. Simultaneously the car swerved to the side of the road, missing a large tree by inches before coming to a stop on the snowy shoulder.

"What in the *hell* was that for?" the dark voice above her bellowed.

Karen tried to pry the arm from her waist, but it was like steel. "Let me go," she croaked, twisting as much as the arm would allow, which was little.

"And have you run out in that mess?"

She kept twisting, kept grabbing the arm, trying to loosen it. "You can't keep me here...I don't want to be here...kidnapping is a capital offense..." The burst of words ended in a fit of thick coughing that hurt her head, her chest, her stomach.

Brice took advantage of her momentary weakness to reach across her and tug the car door closed. He'd no sooner straightened when, coughing behind closed lips, she reached for the handle again. He returned an arm to her waist and pinned her back against the seat.

"I am not kidnapping you," he said in an angry growl.

Karen felt trembly and weak. Her voice reflected it. "I want to get out."

"Not now. Not here."

Head against the headrest, eyes on the road, she was panting shallowly. "Then where?"

"My house."

Her eyes flew to his in alarm. It was the first time she'd viewed him head-on, and if she'd been intimidated before, when she'd thought him a stranger, she was even more so now. Recognition was instantaneous. It didn't matter how many months had passed. She'd never forget those dark, piercing eyes.

Swallowing hard, she tried to sink deeper into the seat of the car, but plush as the leather was, it only gave so much. She held still, very still, suddenly afraid to move or speak.

"You know who I am?" he probed in that same deep voice, but less angrily. He had no qualms about frightening her; she deserved that. Terrorizing her was another story.

She nodded.

"You passed out back there."

She stared at him silently.

"I'd say you're sick," his tone hardened, "so your visiting Rowena was a really dumb thing to do. Do you know how dangerous it would be for her to catch something at her age?"

Again Karen nodded.

Very slowly, Brice withdrew the bond of his arm. There was no further need to physically restrain her. The force of his gaze did that on its own. "So why did you have to see her today? You didn't develop that cough this afternoon. It sounds like it's been in your chest for a while. Didn't it occur to you to skip a visit, or did you think she depended solely on you for human companionship?"

His sarcasm cut into Karen nearly as sharply as the accusation itself. She knew she'd been selfish. If Rowena got sick she'd never forgive herself. Still, she'd needed to come, and the need was her own more than Rowena's. But could she explain that to Brice?

"I was wrong," she admitted quietly, hoarsely. She didn't move other than to take those short breaths, and she wasn't taking her eyes from Brice. She didn't know him. Though they'd seen each other before, this was the very first time they'd talked. He had good reason to hate her. If he wanted revenge, she was in poor shape to defend herself.

"Is that all you have to say?"

"I don't feel well. If you could take me back to my car..." She swallowed the rest of the thought in a lump as the facts of the situation settled on her shoulders. Her car was dead. She was sick. A snowstorm was in full blow. And Brice Carlin was, theoretically, in a position to do with her as he wished. "A cab," she whispered because it took less effort. "There must be one." But the cab fare to Syracuse would be prohibitive. "Or the bus stop. If you could just drop me—"

"Your car?"

"It died."

"That's why you were going back into the nursing home?"

She nodded, feeling suddenly stranded and very cold. Earlier she'd been shaking with fear. That had stopped when Brice's identity had sunk in. He was Rowena's grandson. He wouldn't physically harm her. When she began to tremble now, it was from a chill.

Brice shot a glance at the road, then looked back at Karen and spoke in the slow, deliberate tone of one expecting obedience. "I am going to start driving again." Very carefully, he shifted into gear. "I don't want you to reach for the door because if it opens again and I don't catch you on time, you could get yourself killed." With a look over his shoulder, he pulled back onto the road. "Or you could get both of us killed if I have to swerve off the road again. In case you hadn't noticed, the driving is tricky."

She said nothing because she was feeling dizzy

again. So she closed her eyes and tried to take slow, even breaths. But her chest hurt with each one.

"Put your head between your knees."

"I can't."

He raised his voice to a tone of greater command. "Put your head between your knees."

"It takes too much effort." She was beginning to shiver more noticeably.

"How long have you been this way?"

"Not long."

"*How long?*"

She opened her eyes, thinking that her head would be better if she could see the world. "A week, maybe a little longer." She could see the world, all right, but it wasn't one she recognized. "Are you taking me back to the nursing home?"

"What would be the point of that? The only thing you'd accomplish there would be to infect a few more innocent people."

His words stung, but Karen was feeling too weak to hurt as much as she might otherwise have. "I was careful with Rowena."

"You instructed the germs to behave?"

Sinking lower in the seat, she turned slightly to rest her hot cheek against the leather. "Yes. Are you taking me to a bus?"

"You won't get a bus in this weather. Things are closing down right and left. I told you, I'm taking you to my house, which is about five minutes from here." When she made a sound of protest, he added, "It's either my house or a hospital."

Karen wrapped her arms around her middle in a futile attempt to still the shakes. "I can't afford a hospital."

"I know," he said, but she didn't hear. She had curled into herself, feeling sick and confused. He glanced at her face, what little of it showed above the collar of her coat. Her skin was ashen and damp with sweat. She was clearly sick. He would have no idea how sick until he got her home and took a look. If he decided then that she needed the hospital he wouldn't hesitate to take her there.

For the duration of the drive, Karen drifted in a state of semiawareness. She vacillated between fearing Brice as Rowena's grandson and finding comfort in that fact, but for the most part he was relegated to the periphery of her consciousness. She didn't have the strength to bring him forward, when her primary thought was of escape from her body's misery.

Five minutes stretched to ten when Brice slowed the car to avoid skidding on the ice that slicked the roads. He began to worry. The sensible thing, he knew, would have been to have carried Karen into the nursing home when she'd collapsed. If he had an accident with her in the car, he'd be in trouble.

But he'd come too far to turn back. His house would do fine, he supposed. And after all, he and Karen weren't *total* strangers.

Turning off the main road at last, he directed the car down the short drive and was relieved when the familiar shape of his home emerged through the driving snow. He worked his way carefully over the accumulation on the circular drive and came to a halt immediately in front of the door.

Karen was shivering in her sleep.

Hitching his collar higher, he forged out in the snow, circled the car to the passenger's side, opened the door and lifted her with ease, as he'd done earlier. In several long strides, he was at the front door, then inside.

Karen stirred when he shifted position to kick the door shut behind them. She stared groggily at the oak of the entry hall ceiling, then at Brice, and her eyes widened a fraction. "You can let me down," she whispered hoarsely.

Ignoring her, he entered the larger front hall, crossed directly to the living room and deposited her on a sofa. She immediately put her feet on the floor and sat up.

A cab, she thought. She should call a cab. She looked around the room for a phone, but there was none and she didn't have the strength to go in search of one just yet. She was very cold. Her hands and feet felt like ice, and her insides were shaking. Only by clenching her jaw did she keep her teeth from chattering.

Brice, meanwhile, had tossed his overcoat onto a chair and was hunkered down before the huge fireplace arranging logs for a fire.

Even without the dark topcoat he was intimidating, Karen realized. It could have been his size; he was above average in height, lean but solid. It could have been his clothing; he wore navy slacks and a navy sweater, with only a pale gray shirt collar showing to lighten the effect. It could have been the aura of command he exuded; he placed each log with confidence, almost casually tossed kindling between them, touched a match to the wood and the fire caught.

Probably, she decided, it was his face. Stern. Brooding. Craggy in the way of a man in his prime who had seen—or chosen to see—the dark side of life too often.

She would have wondered about that had she been given the time, but Brice was rising and turning to her with his hands on his hips and annoyance in his eyes.

Karen did her best not to cower, but that became harder as the minutes passed with no sound breaking the silence but the snap and hiss of the growing flame and her own faintly rattling breath. She still wore her coat, scarf and mittens, so her shaking wasn't visible, but for good measure she clamped her hands between her thighs. When Brice continued to stare at her, she averted her gaze. Like a magnet, though, he drew her back before she'd gone far.

She cleared her throat. "I'll be on my way as soon as the snow stops."

The hard lines of his mouth barely yielded when he spoke. "It won't be letting up before morning, and only then if we're lucky. I wouldn't count on the roads being clear for a while."

"A while?" she echoed in a raspy voice as she realized the extent of her predicament. "But...but I can't stay here."

Brice dropped his hands from his hips. "It looks like you haven't got much choice." He reached for his coat. "I'm going to put the car in the garage. I have no intention of driving again."

"You were on your way to see Rowena."

"She wasn't expecting me. She won't worry."

"But I can't stay here." She darted a worried glance at the approximate spot where her watch would be, under her layers of clothing. "I'm supposed to be back in Syracuse. I have to work, and after that I have a paper to write. I *can't* stay here."

Brice studied her for a minute more. Beneath the layers of wool, she was sick, trembling, cold, exhausted and weak, which was all pretty pathetic in his estimation. And still she argued.

But if she thought she could win her case this time, she was mistaken.

With a mirthless smile, he shrugged. "You can't leave." Calmly pulling up his collar, he left the room.

2

Karen didn't like that smile. She didn't like the tone of voice. She didn't like the man.

True, he was Rowena's grandson, and she trusted that he wouldn't cause her harm, but there was harm and there was harm. It didn't take a genius to interpret that smile. Brice Carlin might not take a hand to her physically, but that smile said he wouldn't be averse to a little psychological torture.

Karen wasn't sitting still for any kind of torture.

Inching to the edge of the sofa, she took a breath and pushed herself to her feet. She found her shaky way back to the hall, crossed it and entered a room that was the twin of the other. There she began to feel dizzy. So she rested a hip against the worn leather sofa and bowed her head until the brief wave had passed, then moved on into the next room. It boasted more of the same dark woodwork, including an elegant mahogany table and chairs, and was clearly the dining room. Crossing through that, she reached a huge butler's pantry and, finally, the kitchen.

A telephone sat on the tiled countertop. Lifting the receiver, she called directory assistance, and within a minute was talking with an agent at the bus station.

Brice was right. Nothing was running.

Desperate, she placed another call, this one to the dispatcher of one of the local cab companies. His language was more colorful than the bus station attendant's had been, but the message was the same.

"They're not crazy," Brice said from the door. Glassy-eyed, Karen turned in time to see him toss his gloves to the counter. Crystals of snow dotted his hair and shoulders. "They wouldn't be caught dead out there."

Which was pretty much what the dispatcher had said. "I'll try another company," she said and coughed.

"Try five. You won't get anywhere. The roads are treacherous. Visibility is next to nil."

She pressed the phone to her ear and squeezed her eyes shut. "Some driver has to want the money badly enough." But when she opened her eyes to dial another number, she found that the world had tilted. She swayed and caught herself on the edge of the counter. In the process she dropped the phone.

Brice smoothly scooped it up and set it in its cradle, but his smoothness faltered when he turned back to Karen. She was wearing an expression so helpless that the healer in him was pricked.

"I think," he said in a lordly voice, "that you ought to lie down by the fire." He curved a large hand around her upper arm and took a step, only to stop when she didn't move. He looked down at her. He gave a small tug with his hand.

Karen returned to the living room with him, not because she was giving up the fight but because she

knew when to regroup. He was right. She ought to
lie down by the fire, at least until she warmed up. She
was so cold. So hot. So tired. Besides, there were no
buses running. No cabbies were willing to pick her
up. She'd tried.

Her knees gave way just as she lowered herself to
the sofa. Unable to help herself, she leaned sideways
until her head hit the armrest, which was soft, covered
in the same plush corduroy as the rest of the piece.
She barely noticed when Brice raised her legs, but
quickly curled them beneath her in a bid for warmth.

A cool hand felt her forehead, her cheek. A brusque
voice said, "You're burning up."

"I'm cold."

"That's the fever. Don't move. I'll be back."

Karen didn't care whether he returned or not. She
had withdrawn into herself and was concentrating
once more on escaping the misery. Sleep wasn't coming so quickly this time, though. She opened her eyes
to see the fire, closed them to see sparks behind her
lids. She tucked her hands between her knees, shifted
a little, moaned.

Then Brice was back, unwrapping the scarf from
her neck.

She clamped a hand to the scarf. "Don't do that.
I'm cold."

"Your things are damp from the snow," he said
tightly. "I have blankets. You'll be warmer in them."

Something of what he said made sense. Karen removed her hand from the scarf and was about to lift
her head to help him when he did it for her. Gently,

firmly, efficiently. In the same manner, he removed her mittens, then her coat. She was sitting up by this time, feeling awkward and not so much cold as hot. Brice was squatting before her, tugging at her high boots.

"I can do that," she insisted, but feebly, and he had the boots off before she could muster the strength.

Closing a hand around her foot, which felt cold even through the wool tights she wore, he looked up at her. "How long did you say this has been going on?"

She lifted one shoulder in a shrug. "A little while."

"How little a while?"

"A week. Maybe two."

He was studying her eyes in a strange way. She was trying to figure out what he saw there when he suddenly raised his hand and began to touch her neck.

With a hoarse cry, she shrank out of his reach. "What are you doing?"

"Checking for swollen glands. Did that hurt?"

"I don't know."

He shifted to sit on the sofa, and his hand was back, fingers probing efficiently, before Karen could escape. "Hurt?"

"No!" she protested, then promptly started to cough. When she'd caught her breath, she said, "Persistent, aren't you? Where did you get your medical degree? Sears and Roebuck?"

Brice dropped his hand and said stiffly, "Yale, actually. Then Sloan-Kettering."

Karen's jaw dropped.

He was almost as surprised. "You didn't know I was a doctor?"

She shook her head.

"Rowena never told you?"

She shook her head again.

He frowned. "How much *do* you know about me?"

"Just that you're Rowena's grandson, that you visit her often and that you have no cause to like me."

"Right on all three counts," he said, then narrowed an eye. "And she never said I was a doctor?"

Karen wanted to lie down again. Her head felt like lead, her eyes like hot pokers, her chest like a trough of mud, her stomach like quicksand. "I've answered that twice," she said, and not caring that Brice was sitting right there, keeled over and curled up. She broke into several deep, hacking coughs, then murmured weakly, "I don't understand it." Her eyes were closed, one arm thrown over her face. "It was a cold. Just a cold."

"When did it start?"

"Three weeks ago."

"*Three.*"

"It's been coming and going ever since."

"Did you pamper it at all?"

She didn't answer at first. Her breathing was audible over the crackle of the flames. Finally she said, "I tried taking naps, but I couldn't sleep."

"You must have stayed home from school."

She shifted, moaned, murmured, "How do you know I go to school?"

Brice propped his elbows on his knees, but there was nothing casual about his expression. His features were hard. "I know you go to school because I did some snooping when I found out you were visiting my grandmother. You're a second-semester freshman. You're on half-scholarship. You pay the rest by doing research for Arnold McGuire and waiting tables at the Pepper Mill."

Karen suddenly felt exposed. She began to shake again. "You said you had blankets," she whispered, not looking at Brice. Within moments, a light weight covered her body, then a second weight joined the first. Still she trembled.

If she'd been sitting up, facing him, showing the slightest semblance of strength, Brice might have continued his questioning. But she was such a miserable figure that he couldn't. Without thinking beyond warming her up, he began to rub her back. She tried to escape his touch at first, but when his hand persisted in following her, she gave in.

She was too thin, Brice realized. He'd caught sight of her on other occasions when she'd visited Rowena and she'd always given the impression of slenderness. Now he felt it with his hands. He chafed her back, slowed the pace to rub her arms and legs. He wondered how much weight she'd lost to her illness.

"Are you taking any medicine?" he asked evenly.

She didn't answer. Seconds later, she sent him a dazed frown and croaked, "I didn't...did you ask something?"

"Are you taking any medicine?"

"Mmm." In a thin, cracked voice she listed an antihistamine, a nasal spray and a cough syrup by brand. All were over-the-counter remedies that, Brice knew, were akin to putting a finger in the dyke.

"When did you take them last?"

She was drifting in and out. "This morning—no, noon—mmm, before I left to see Rowena."

He continued his rubbing until her tremors had eased. Then he felt her cheek with the back of his hand and rose from the sofa. Several minutes later, he was back.

"Karen?" He pushed a tangle of hair from her forehead.

With effort, she opened her eyes.

"I have to know your temperature. Can you put this under your tongue?"

Obediently she opened her mouth, then closed it on the cool, slim instrument.

"Have you seen a doctor at all?"

She made a small, negative movement with her head.

"Are you taking any medication other than what you just told me?"

She repeated the negative gesture.

"Has there been any nausea along with the cold?" No.

"You've had dizziness, though. Any fainting spells before today?"

No.

"Are you pregnant?"

The headshake came a little faster this time. With

the thermometer still in her mouth, she coughed, then winced and pressed her head to the cushions.

"That hurt?"

She gave a single nod.

"Your head or your chest?" She was trying to figure out how to answer when he simplified things by asking, "Both?"

She nodded.

He left her alone for a minute, and she gratefully faded out. Then he was back, this time disturbing the blankets. She yielded the thermometer to Brice just before he drew her sweater over her head. Then she fell back to the sofa and looked up at him. She might have protested had she not been feeling warm again. The air felt good on her neck, and her pullover had been too warm anyway.

"Is it hot in here, or is it me?" she asked in a raw whisper.

"It's you," Brice answered. He flicked open the first few buttons of her blouse, warmed the stethoscope on his thigh for a second, then slid it against her skin. When he'd heard enough, he flicked open two more buttons and eased the blouse away from her shoulders to gain access to her back. At length, he folded the instrument and set it aside. Then he drew the blankets back to her chin.

Karen waited for him to speak. As disoriented as she felt, she sensed something in his silence, and along with the sensing came fear. To be examined by a doctor was to admit to sickness, but she didn't have the time to be sick. She couldn't *afford* to be sick.

But she was. On top of whatever germ lurked in her body, she was overworked, overtired, over-wrought. It wasn't fair, when she was trying so hard to do it all and succeed. And she thought she *had* been succeeding—until now. Suddenly her world seemed to be caving in.

Unable to help herself, she began to cry.

Brice hadn't expected that. She'd been remarkably composed up to then. He'd thought her too hard for tears. But there they came, trickling down her cheeks with the slow cadence of near-silent sobs.

His first thought was that she wanted something, that she was playing on his sympathy to achieve her own ends. But there was something about the way she was hiding her head, shrinking into herself as though she were mortified. She looked very uncomfortable, very unhappy and very alone.

He could identify with all three.

"You'll be okay," he assured her gruffly. He raised a hand to stroke her hair but stopped short and, instead, cupped her shoulder. "There's no need for a hospital. I can treat you myself."

He had no idea if she heard him. The soft crying continued.

Feeling oddly helpless, he moved his hand to her back and began to rub it as he'd been doing earlier. "It's all right, Karen. You'll be fine once you've had the right medication and some rest."

She sniffled and used her hands to wipe the tears.

"Are you allergic to penicillin?"

"No," she whispered without looking at him.

"You've had it before?"

She gave a quick nod.

"Good," he said. His hand had stopped on her shoulder. He gave it a squeeze, then rose from the sofa and left the room.

Without knowing why, Karen started crying again, but she regained control of herself sooner this time and, other than the intermittent cough, was lying quietly when he returned.

"I'm going to give you a shot," he said, moving the blankets only as much as was necessary. "That way the medicine will get into your system faster."

She barely felt the sting of the needle. It was lost among the rest of her aches, and even if it hadn't been she would have welcomed anything that promised to bring her relief. When the blankets were tucked around her once more, she settled into them and, with surprising speed, fell asleep.

"Karen?"

She gave a closed-mouth cough.

"Karen?" Brice raised her until she was nearly sitting. "I want you to swallow some aspirin for the fever."

She struggled to open her eyes and whispered a hoarse, "What time is it?"

"Dinnertime," he said in that same low voice that wasn't quite hostile, wasn't quite friendly. "Are you hungry?"

She shook her head, opened her mouth to take in

the two tablets he pressed there, then washed them down with several sips of water.

He tapped her bottom lip with the edge of the cup. "Finish it. You need the liquid."

"I have to go to the bathroom."

"When you finish the water."

She finished the water because she was thirsty. Then wrapping the blankets securely over her shoulders, she gripped the edge of the sofa and tried to push herself up, only to lose her balance and sink right back down.

She moaned but held up a hand to stop Brice when he would have lifted her. "I'm okay." This time she made it to her feet and managed to weave halfway across the floor before wavering. Brice was there to catch her.

"If there's one thing I can't stand," he muttered as he carried her through the hall, "it's a bullheaded woman."

"Do you know many?"

He frowned down at her. "My grandmother and you. Two peas in a pod, only *you* can't blame it on senility like she does."

"She's not senile."

"Damn right she's not, but she's wily enough to use it as an excuse." He set her down inside a warmly lit powder room and asked in a voice edged with sarcasm, "Can you manage, or should I stay here and hold you?"

Karen pointed a shaky finger toward the hall. She shut the door firmly the instant he was out, then quickly dropped the blankets and collapsed on the commode.

Brice settled himself on the stairway nearby. It wasn't that he didn't respect Karen's right to privacy, simply that he was worried she'd fall and hurt herself. Not that he cared, on one level. She could hurt herself if she pleased, but on her own time. While she was in his home, she was his responsibility, and he took his responsibilities seriously.

Apparently so did Karen, but she'd gone off the deep end this time. She was weak and shaky, feverish and congested. It galled him that she'd gone to visit Rowena in that condition. Then again, it amazed him that she'd been able to pull it off. Sheer willpower must have kept her on her feet.

Sheer willpower, he didn't mind. He respected independence. Same thing with determination. But he had little patience with bullheadedness. Karen had been crazy not to pay attention to her health. She must have suspected that she had more than a cold when she was still feeling lousy after two weeks. Nevertheless, she hadn't taken time off from school, she hadn't taken time off from work, she hadn't seen a doctor...and she'd continued to visit Rowena.

His features darkened each time he thought of that. She had no business risking Rowena's health. He wondered why she had. Was it selfishness? Or bullheadedness, a refusal to admit she was sick? Or was it guilt that brought her two times a week, week after week to Rowena's side?

The bathroom door opened slowly. Karen emerged

holding tightly to the knob with one hand, to the blankets with the other. Her face was damp, as though she'd splashed it with water, and the wet tendrils of hair that framed it gave her a fragile look. In the dim light of the hall the shadows beneath her eyes were more pronounced. Wrappings and all, she looked as if a gust of wind would blow her over.

Brice Carlin was a sucker for people in need. He'd always been that way, which was why he found his profession so rewarding. When people were sick, they were in need. When they came to him, he did everything in his power to treat the need, heal the wound, cure the illness. It wasn't always possible, and those cases made him ache. The thought of his grandmother, once such an active woman, now sidelined, made him ache. He couldn't cure her ills, and she fought him right and left, which didn't help.

Karen wasn't fighting him—at least not at the moment. Swathed in a mass of blankets, with only her head showing above and her stockinged feet showing beneath, she was looking at him as though she was lost and in need of direction. Moreover, she seemed to be relying on him for that direction and would be willing to do whatever he said.

It should have been heady, that sense of power, particularly feeling it over Karen Drew. Strangely, though, it wasn't as satisfying as he would have thought.

Rising from the stairs, he approached her. "Everything okay?"

She nodded. He saw the tremor at her shoulders that said she was shivering.

"Want to go back in the living room?"

She nodded again.

He didn't wait for her to crumple this time. Nor did he lift her from the ground. Rather, he curved an arm around her waist and provided the little bit of extra steam she needed to walk.

Once back on the living room sofa, she immediately put down her head and closed her eyes. Brice was standing there just looking at her when she said in a small, nasal voice, "They were expecting me at the Pepper Mill. I have to call."

"I'll do it."

Eyes still closed, she gave a single short nod. She didn't thank him, nor did she offer the number, but Brice didn't expect either. He knew that she was totally drained and could well imagine the energy it took for her to speak.

Without another word, he went into the kitchen and called the restaurant. Then he made himself a sandwich, poured a glass of milk and carried both back into the living room to eat before the fire.

Exhausted, Karen slept through his meal, but it was a fitful sleep. She didn't thrash around; she was too weak for that. Rather, she moved an arm, then rested, moved a leg, then rested, turned her head on the armrest, rested, coughed, rested, inched the blankets higher on her neck.

Brice watched her. He thought back to how he'd picked her up from the snow, and though technically it all made sense, there was something odd about her being in his home. Part of it was that he wasn't used to having a woman around. He wasn't used to having anyone around. He was a solitary man, a man who, after hours, liked his home and his time to himself.

He didn't feel like reading a book now, though. He didn't feel like listening to music or proofing the article he'd written or watching a basketball game. He felt like sitting and watching Karen.

Which was what was so strange. Karen Drew. Of all people. That she was in his living room, huddled beneath blankets on his sofa, entrusting herself to his care was incredible. That he had invited her to do so was even more bizarre.

She came to with a start. She gasped, coughed, peered at him over a corner of the blanket, then dropped her head and fell back to sleep.

"Karen?" He lowered the blanket from her face to find that her cheeks were still flushed, her skin hot. Settling on the edge of the sofa, he propped her up against his chest. "More aspirin."

Her eyes flickered. They didn't exactly open, but he sensed she saw something because she opened her mouth just when he reached it with the pills.

"Another shot?" she asked in a scratchy whisper after the pills were gone.

"You slept through it."

She seemed content with that. "What time is it?"

"Eleven."

She did come to life then, opening her eyes wide, struggling to sit up on her own. "Eleven at night?"

The darkness of the room attested to it. The flame in the hearth provided the sole light. "Is it still snowing?"

"Yes."

With a whimper, she sank back against him. "I have to get home."

"Not tonight, you don't."

"I can't *stay* here."

"I thought we settled that."

With another whimper, she rolled toward the back of the sofa, where she murmured to the thick corduroy, "I have so much to do. I can't stay. I can't."

Brice's patience began to wane. "You can't go anywhere until the snow ends and the roads are cleared."

"If I were home, I could work on my paper."

"Uh-uh. You're sick."

"I could still work," she argued. Her voice was distant, its throaty sound absorbed by the corduroy. "I could bundle myself up in bed and write."

"How would you do that," he asked sharply, "when you can't keep your head up for more than five seconds at a stretch?"

"I could do it."

He considered the possibility, then said with disdain, "I suppose you could. It's probably nothing more than you've been doing for the past three weeks. Tell me. How much sleep do you get a night?" When she shrugged, he prodded. "How much?"

She shrugged again, but this time she followed it up with a subdued, "Five hours, maybe."

"And you think that's enough? Hasn't it occurred to you that you may be run-down? That if you'd taken care of yourself when you'd first caught cold, you'd be fine now?"

Karen's will to argue was petering out. "You sound like a doctor."

"I *am* a doctor."

"And a self-righteous one at that," she mumbled, but he heard it.

Rising to his feet, he stared down at her back. "Self-righteous or not, I'm right, and if you have any brains, little lady, you'll admit it. You may be great at jam-packing your life with a million and one things to do, but there comes a time when you have to slow down, and if you can't see that, you're in big trouble." Bent on getting the last word, he strode from the room, but by the time he reached the kitchen, he was growling to himself.

"Bullheaded woman." He grabbed a saucepan, filled it with water and put it on the stove none too gently. As soon as the gas was dancing beneath it, he opened a nearby cabinet. "Why do I waste my breath? She won't listen. She'll do the same thing again." He put a large mug on the counter. "And so what if she does? It's no sweat off my back. What in the hell is she to me?" Taking a tea bag from a cannister, he tossed it into the mug, then raised both hands in surrender. "Want to kill yourself, go ahead. I'm not your keeper."

Karen didn't respond, of course. Back in the living room, she couldn't hear a word he said. She was fully awake, though, and aware of how awful she felt—most immediately, how hot. Pushing the blankets aside, she sat up and plucked her blouse from her sweat-dampened skin. It was already free of her skirt, but the skirt was a heavy wool number that was at the moment unwanted. So she pushed it off her hips and out of the way.

Her blouse covered her from neck to thigh, her wool tights from waist to toe. Folding her legs Indian-style with the blouse draped sedately between, she sat forward. The change of position felt nice for a minute, but she was still too warm.

So she put a hand to her hair. The long curls that she'd secured from crown to nape in a series of barrettes had long since escaped their bonds. Removing the barrettes, she combed her fingers through the way-ward tangles, lifted them and let them fall over the top of the sofa as she sat back. Then, hands lying limply by her hips, she closed her eyes and tried to think cool.

That was how Brice found her when he returned. He was carrying the mug of tea, expecting that she'd be lying as he'd left her with her back to the fire, and he came to a sudden halt when he saw it wasn't so.

For a minute he simply stood there. She was an elf in loden green, wispy and petite. She was also sexy as hell, but the instant he heard the thought, he denied it. She wasn't sexy; she was sick.

Armed with that deliberate reminder, he continued into the room. Karen didn't move until he crossed in front of the fire, alerting her to his presence. Whether it was his shadow or the deflection of heat with his passing, he didn't know, but she opened her eyes, stared at him blankly for a minute, then suddenly realized what she was wearing and how she was sitting. Quick as a flash, she shifted her weight, brought her legs together and grabbed the blanket.

"I was hot," she murmured without looking at him. Homing in on one of the barrettes she'd discarded, she gathered her hair and shakily secured it into a high ponytail.

Brice set the tea on the end table within easy reach of her hand and said, "Drink this." Then he hunkered down by the hearth and added another log to the fire. "It may make you sweat more, but it'll loosen up what's in your chest."

Karen cast a dubious glance at the mug and asked quietly, "Is it poison?"

"I didn't have the guts."

"Then it must be tea. Almost as bad." Turning sideways, she drew her knees in and covered them with the blanket. "I've had so much tea in the past three weeks that I should be sprouting tags."

Brice found the thought vaguely amusing, but he didn't crack a smile. He had other things on his mind. Swiveling, he faced her. "I wasn't trying to be self-righteous before. I was trying to get across the message that if you hope to get better, you'll have to take a breather from that schedule of yours."

She moved her cheek against the sofa and fiddled with the blanket binding. "What's wrong with me?" she asked almost idly.

"Bronchial pneumonia, I'd guess."

She closed her eyes, only then aware that she'd been frightened. She'd lived through years of illness with her parents, but bronchial pneumonia wasn't so bad. "Are you sure?"

Brice frowned. "Were you expecting something else?"

"No," she answered quickly. "I just wondered."

"I don't think you have cause for worry. Assuming," he added sternly, "that you take care of yourself. This looks like a classic case. I can't know for sure unless you're X-rayed, and I don't have the equipment here. If the penicillin works, it won't be necessary."

"How long will it take to work?"

"A day, maybe two."

She tipped back her head, closed her eyes and whispered, "Two days. Oh, hell."

Her head lowered, but her eyes stayed shut. Brice thought of reminding her that it was a weekend, that she couldn't have picked a better time to be sick, that by the first of the week she'd be feeling a whole lot better, but he thought twice and remained still. She would argue that her weekends were precious, that she had to work at the restaurant, that she had to write her paper. He remembered the grind. He'd been through it himself. But that had been when he'd been young and pompous, when he'd felt he was God's gift to the ill.

When had he changed, and why? He wasn't sure. It hadn't been anything traumatic, simply the passage of time, the reaching of maturity. Somewhere in his early thirties—just about the age Karen was reaching—he'd realized that there was more to life than work. That was when he'd bought his home and set up shop in Ithaca, when he'd rediscovered books and music, when he'd begun to travel.

It was also when he'd learned about loneliness.

Taking the chair not far from the sofa, he slid low in it, extended his legs, crossed his ankles, folded his hands on his chest and watched Karen sleep.

It was nearly two in the morning when she awoke. The room was darker than before. The fire had burned down to a layer of smoldering embers that could barely produce enough heat to warm the room. That didn't bother her, though. She was burning up again, dripping with sweat. Pushing the blanket aside, she sat up, only to lie right back down when her head protested the sudden movement. It was from that position that she looked for Brice.

He was a long dark form sprawled in the chair.

"Brice?" she whispered, not sure if he was asleep. He didn't answer.

She rose gingerly this time, pushed herself to her feet and crossed the room. After pausing to steady herself at the door, she continued on into the bathroom. Several minutes later, she was leaning heavily against the sink with a wet towel over her eyes when a knock came at the door, followed closely by an imperative, "Are you all right?"

Blindly she reached for the door and pulled it open. "I'm okay," she croaked.

Brice took one look at the way she was standing— as though the only things keeping her upright were a pair of locked knees and the sink—and eased her down to the toilet seat. Her head and shoulder came to rest against his hip with something akin to finality.

"You should have woken me," he said—irritably, because he felt bad and didn't want to.

She gave the tiniest of headshakes against his hip.

"How long have you been up?" he asked.

"A couple of minutes."

"Don't feel so hot?"

"I feel *too* hot. That's the problem."

Brice saw the way strands of hair were plastered to her neck. He brushed his fingers under the back collar of her blouse; the skin there was wet with sweat. "Has the towel helped?"

"A little."

"Want to sponge off more?"

"I want a bath."

He tried to decide whether it was petulance he heard or simply bluntness. He supposed it didn't matter. "Do you feel strong enough?"

"It doesn't take strength to lie in a tub."

"It does if you want to keep from drowning."

She moaned. "Maybe I'll just go back to sleep."

Brice let her consider the options for a minute, during which time she coughed once but didn't otherwise move. He leaned forward to see if she'd fallen asleep.

"Karen?"

After a minute, she gave a nasal, "Hmm?"

"I'm taking you upstairs. There's a bath. And a bed."

"Not yours," she said with surprising fierceness.

"No."

Her fierceness vanished. "Okay."

Slipping an arm beneath her knees and one around her back, he carried her into the hall, then up the winding stairs. There were four spare bedrooms, only one of which was furnished. He took her there. With only the lamp from the hall to light his way, he set her gently on the four-poster bed. Then he entered the adjoining bathroom and ran a warm bath before returning for her.

And it hit him again. Something about her as she sat on the edge of the bed. Something that touched him for no apparent reason.

Women didn't usually touch him, not in the emotional sense. But Karen did.

Unsurely she turned her head to him. Then, painstakingly, she got up from the bed and crossed to the bathroom. He stood aside.

"Can you handle it?" he asked without a trace of sarcasm.

She nodded.

"Yell if there's a problem."

Again she nodded, then shut the door.

Frowning, Brice went to the window. The room looked out on the front of the house, the circular drive, the short road to the street. A lamppost stood at the point where the road met the drive. It was lit.

He left it lit all night, every night, a sign that he was home if someone needed him.

Tonight it lit a particularly beautiful scene. Snow was still falling, blanketing not only the lawn but the surrounding stands of juniper, hemlock and pine. The light bathed them gently, the effect was one of charm, of peace.

Taking a bit of that peace inside him, he went to the bed, drew back the hand-quilted coverlet, straightened the pillow. He glanced at the small line of light that escaped from beneath the bathroom door, listened, heard nothing. So he called, "Are you okay, Karen?"

"Uh-huh," came her weak reply.

For another minute he stood with his hands on his hips, wondering what he could do. Then he left the room and went down the hall to his own, where he found the largest, softest shirt he owned.

Back at the bathroom door, he called, "Still awake?"

"Uh-huh," came the same weak reply.

After several minutes, he heard a splash, then the soft rush of water down the drain. Bracing his back against the wall, he waited for her to dry off, then waited through an even longer period of total silence. Finally it was broken by the hesitant call of his name.

He opened the door to find her wrapped in a towel, sitting on the edge of the tub. Her face was washed out, her tired eyes sending him a frantic message. Her shoulders were bare, very pale, very thin. And she was shaking.

Wishing he could say something sharp about helpless women but unable to utter a word, he helped her into the shirt, buttoning it down to her thighs before tugging the towel from underneath. Then he scooped her up and put her in bed before returning to tidy the bathroom.

When he emerged, she was sleeping. He touched her skin; it was cooler than before. He brushed several long, wispy curls from her cheek, ran his thumb very, very lightly over the line of her jaw to her chin. He took a spare blanket from the closet and layered it over the quilt. Then, leaving a slim sliver of light coming from the bathroom and the door to the hall open, he returned to his room to lie awake for hours trying to summon up suitable contempt for Karen Drew.

3

Karen had been driving the car that had hit Rowena two years before. The night had been dark, the road narrow. Rowena had had no business riding a bicycle without reflectors at that time of night, Karen's lawyer had argued, and the judge had agreed. Allegations that Karen had been speeding had been impossible to prove.

Brice had been furious.

His fury had toned down some since the day of the verdict, but it had far from disappeared. He knew that he couldn't blame Karen for Rowena's stroke, but he blamed her for most else, which was why he'd been livid the month before, when he'd arrived to visit Rowena and first seen Karen there. He'd raised hell with the administrators of the home, particularly when they told him Karen had been a regular visitor since shortly after Rowena had arrived. He'd gone so far as to forbid them to let her in again, but they'd calmly told him that the matter wasn't his to decide. Rowena was in the nursing home by her own choice and at her own expense. Hardest to accept was their claim that Rowena looked forward to Karen's visits, though he could almost believe it—his grandmother was a sunny, forgiving sort.

He was not.
He had to remember that.

Karen slept soundly for a time, then more fitfully as dawn approached. She coughed often, coughs that shook her slender frame from within and left her weak. She was more comfortable in bed, where the sheets were smooth and cool against her skin, and the large shirt she wore was a definite improvement over a sweaty blouse and wool tights, but her head felt twice its normal size, and the rest of her ached.

She was aware of the occasional ring of a distant phone and of Brice's periodic, professional ministrations. He left the room dark and rarely spoke, and when he did he said little, which was fine with her, as she wasn't up to talking.

Even through the haze of her illness, though, she thought him a contradiction. He didn't like her, and with good reason. Yet while his voice was cool, his hands were gentle. He was conscientious in his care of her, and she couldn't imagine why. She couldn't imagine why he hadn't left her lying in the snow the afternoon before.

It was late in the morning when she awoke for more than a groggy minute or two. Shifting position, she raised an arm to sweep her ponytail off her neck and left her wrist propped limply on her head as she looked around the room. For the first time she registered the early American charm of its decor, but that was an overall impression. She didn't have time to examine the details because Brice caught her eye.

He was sitting in a wooden rocker, not rocking, just staring. It seemed the simplest thing for her to stare right back.

He was a very serious man. His hair was dark and on the long side. His eyes were dark also, though she couldn't tell their color over the distance. His features had a ruggedness to them that seemed somehow mismatched with the preppiness of his clothes—a fresh version of the shirt, sweater and cords he'd worn the day before.

She guessed him to be forty, though whether the stoniness of his expression made him look older than he actually was she didn't know. Etched into that stone was a crease between his eyes. He was a very serious man, indeed.

The very serious man spoke. "How do you feel?"

"Okay," she said in a strained non-sound.

"That tells me nothing, and you sound like hell. Do you feel better or worse?"

She thought about that for a minute. "Better, I guess. My bones don't hurt as much." The gaze she turned to the window grew worried. "It's still snowing, isn't it?"

"Yes."

"The roads haven't been plowed?"

"They have—several times—but it keeps piling up."

"Maybe the next time the plows come around—"

He knew just what she was thinking, could see it in the slight, hopeful rise of her brows. He was quick to set her straight. "The plows can't help you. They don't come near the house, and my own man won't be by until the snow stops."

"But you're a doctor," she argued in that same would-be voice. "You have to get out."

"My office is here."

"Then patients have to get in."

"They know to try the hospital in weather like this. If there was a severe emergency, the police would come for me."

She closed her eyes and swallowed hard, then looked at the ceiling. "I can't stay here all day." She dropped her gaze to his relentlessly unwavering one. "You can't want me to stay."

"You're wasting your voice."

"I'm the *last* person you want in your home."

Brice's expression was grim. "I don't have any more choice in the matter than you do. I can't turn off the snow. In fact, the snow just turned off the electricity, so now the town crews have something else to worry about besides plowing."

Karen greeted that news with a look of despair, but she didn't say anything. Talking was a definite effort. Sinking deeper into the pillow, she closed her eyes and thought of her apartment in Syracuse, thought of the books waiting on her desk, thought of her job at the Pepper Mill and wondered if they'd hold it for her when she failed to show two days in a row. Rolling to her side, she gave a helpless moan and clutched her stomach.

Brice's hand was on her forehead nearly before the moan had died. She was still warm, but not as hot as she'd been. He hadn't expected the beads of sweat that suddenly dotted her nose.

Concerned in spite of himself, he asked, "What is it?"

"Nothing," she whispered.

"Are you feeling worse?"

She didn't answer.

"Karen."

"It's my mind," she mumbled.

"Explain that."

She opened her eyes to his and wondered if a man like him, a man who seemed to be totally controlled, could possibly understand. "When I think about everything I should be doing, I get an awful feeling. Like something's holding me down, smothering me. Like something's inside trying to get out. Antsy. Almost panicky."

Brice understood, all right, but rather than launch into a repeat of his repent-or-suffer speech, he straightened. "I haven't got any medicine for that. You're right. It's psychological."

She snorted, then realized the error of that when she started to cough. After she'd caught her breath, she closed her eyes again and whispered, "Don't you have something that can knock me out until the snow stops and I can leave?"

He studied her ashen face. "Is that what you want?"

She was silent, then said in a defeated whisper, "I just want to get up and walk out and go back to doing everything that has to be done."

"Karen, the world will still be there when you recover."

She gave a skeptical "Hmph," which was all she could garner the strength for. She'd zapped herself again.

Sensing that, Brice said, "You must be hungry."

"No more tea," she whispered.

"I was thinking of eggs and toast."

Turning to her other side, she snuggled into the quilt. "Maybe later."

"You should eat."

"Later."

Frowning, he stared at her. Then his frown became a scowl. He felt as though he'd been dismissed. It was a disconcerting feeling, one he didn't particularly like. People didn't usually turn down his services.

Not that he'd offered this particular service to many people. There was Karen, and Rowena. Rowena had refused it, too. That had been years before, when he'd still been in the city, and she'd taken time out from her endless stream of activities to pay him a visit. He'd thought himself rather gallant to have offered, and he'd been hurt when she'd turned him down flat.

"I've seen how you make your eggs, Brice Carlin," she'd said in a knowing tone. "*Hard*. You want them to obey you. You want them to stay just so on the plate. Well, I like my eggs soft. I like them doing their own thing. I like having to chase them a little. Soft eggs make life interesting."

At the time he'd simply scowled and yielded the kitchen to her, but he'd thought about her message afterward and gradually he'd begun to make his eggs softer. Somehow, though, he'd never had the opportunity to offer Rowena breakfast again. She'd been always on the go, and when she visited him, she insisted on taking over his kitchen.

Now, of course, she couldn't do that.

Hardened by the thought, and still annoyed that Karen hadn't jumped at his offer, he headed straight for the kitchen, where he proceeded to cook the breakfast that she was going to eat. When he returned to her room, she was sleeping.

Twice he reached for her, intent on waking her up. Twice he drew back and straightened. Then, glaring at her tucked form, he grabbed the tray from where he'd set it, returned to the kitchen and, with a pithy oath, dumped the soft, perfectly cooked eggs into the sink.

Karen was hungry when she woke up, and Brice was nowhere in sight, which disconcerted her. He had the strangest capacity to make her feel safe. She supposed it was the aura of command he projected. He had certainly taken over when she'd collapsed in the snow, and she had to admit she could have done far worse than landing in a warm house with her own personal physician. It wasn't like he was keeping her there against her wishes. The snow was doing that.

Slowly, she sat up, dropped her feet to the floor and steadied herself, then padded silently to the window. Still snowing. She glanced down at her watch, only to remember she'd left it in the bathroom when she'd bathed. After retrieving it, she looked around.

Her clothes were nowhere in sight or she'd have surely put them on, if only to tell herself she was on her way home. Not that anything she saw out the window suggested she *was* on her way home, but whenever she thought of the time that was passing, she felt that restlessness bordering on panic that she'd described to Brice.

Pushing panic from mind, she straightened in front of the bathroom mirror and took stock of herself. That was even more discouraging, and her legs had begun to wobble, so she returned to the bedroom, this time sliding into the rocking chair Brice had occupied earlier.

Slowly she rocked. Slowly she looked around the room. As prisons went, it was quite charming, she mused. The four-poster was early American, as was the dresser. The quilt on the bed matched the dust ruffle and the drapes, all done in a coordinated variety of small country prints. The colors were mauve and pale blue, and were picked up as solids in a cornice over the window, as well as in the frame of a mirror and those of several small pieces of what looked to be original art.

A decorator had obviously done the room, she decided. Brice was a doctor. He didn't have the time to spend on collecting and placing such things as the matched pitcher and basin that stood on the bureau. She doubted he'd have the inclination, either. He looked to be a clinician, a man who diagnosed and treated, diagnosed and treated, diagnosed and treated, with a slew of paperwork in between. Not an artistic man at all.

Still, the room was lovely. Emotionally warm. Physically cold. She was eyeing the blanket on the bed, wondering if it was worth the effort of getting out of the chair, when Brice appeared at the door.

He took one look at her, and his expression darkened. Striding to the bed, he snatched up the blanket. He didn't ask her to rise; the hand he placed on her arm did it in no uncertain terms. As soon as she was upright, he wrapped the blanket around her, pressed her back into the chair and knelt to tuck the wool around her feet.

"In case you hadn't noticed," he muttered, "the temperature in here is dropping."

Feeling foolish, she said nothing, but he wasn't satisfied with that. So he eyed her accusingly. "You didn't feel cold?"

"A little, but I figured I'd be sweating in another minute." She endured his silent study of her face for a minute before asking, "Where are my clothes?"

"Downstairs."

She waited for him to say that he'd get them for her. When he didn't she asked as sweetly as she could, given the rasping of her voice, "Am I allowed to have them?"

"No."

The sweetness disappeared. "Why not?"

"Because you're sick. If I give you your clothes, you're apt to think you're better and go running out the door, and if you do that, I'll have to go out after you, and it's still snowing.''

Karen eyed him in disbelief. "You're keeping me here by keeping me naked?''

"You're not naked."

"Close to it."

"I know."

He hadn't smiled. The inflection of his voice hadn't varied from its usual evenness, but there was something of a sudden glimmer in his eyes that pricked Karen inside. She decided that the prick was a hunger pang, since that was what she'd felt before, and, besides, she had the sinking feeling that another discussion with Brice about when she could leave would get her nowhere but tired.

She wanted to discuss food—in particular, how she could get a little of it—but she hesitated. She felt like a parasite. She'd taken shelter, warmth, even clothing from Brice, when in essence she was the enemy.

So she simply sat there and looked at him, waiting for him to ask again if she was hungry.''

"How do you feel?'' he asked instead.

"Weak,'' she answered, hoping he'd take the hint.

He didn't. Thrusting a hand in the pocket of his slacks, he asked, "When was the last time you slept as much as this?''

"When I was four months old. According to my mother, I only got up for meals.'' Another hint tossed out.

Another hint missed. "Is your mother still living?''

"No.''

Brice took his hand from his pocket and ran it around the back of his neck. He tried to remember if he'd seen anyone with her during the trial. He didn't think he had. "Do you have any family?"

"No." She paused, asked cautiously, "How about you?"

"Just Rowena."

She tried again. "You live here alone, then? No housekeeper...cook...?"

"A woman comes in on weekdays."

"To cook?" She didn't think she could be more blunt.

"Mostly to clean. I'm not a fussy eater."

"Neither am I," Karen said.

She paused, waited, was just about to give up when Brice informed her, "You really ought to eat. Even if you're not hungry. You have to build yourself up."

"I'm *hungry*," she said without further ado.

His expression turned indignant. "Why didn't you say so?"

"Because I've imposed on you too much already."

"So what's a little more? I think I can spare a couple of eggs."

"A piece of toast will be plenty."

"No, it won't. You're not much more than skin and bones."

"Thanks," she whispered, feeling hurt for no valid reason. She knew she was thin, and Brice had done nothing more than use a common figure of speech. Why she suddenly felt like a living scarecrow—and why it mattered to her—was the puzzlement. She wondered if it had something to do with the contrasting hardiness of his physique.

Eyes averted, she started to rise from the chair. "Actually, I'd be glad to help myself—"

"Sit," Brice growled.

She sat.

"Better still, get back in bed."

But Karen didn't like being ordered around. "I'll sit here," she said with as much dignity as she could muster given the rusty sound of her voice and her ridiculously swathed shape. She did hold her chin steady, and her eyes were firm on his. Apparently she succeeded in conveying the strength of her intent, because after staring at her for several long, silent moments, Brice turned on his heel and left the room.

Only when Karen heard his footsteps recede to a safe enough distance did she get up from the chair and return to bed, which was where he found her when he returned fifteen minutes later. Because she was lying on her side facing the window, she didn't see the way he paused for an instant at the door. Nor did she see the self-satisfied look that passed over his face in that instant. When he suddenly appeared in her line of vision, she slowly raised her eyes.

He gave a short toss of his chin. In response, she struggled up and propped both pillows behind her back. He set the tray across her knees, then stepped away and settled into the rocker to watch her eat.

Unfortunately, her general grogginess didn't prevent her from feeling awkward. She wasn't a performer. She didn't like being the center of attention.

Some people called her shy, and once upon a time that had been true. Now she was simply a private person. She did her own thing, went her own way. Even if she hadn't been too busy to cultivate large groups of friends, that wasn't her style. She was a loner, she supposed even more so of late.

She wasn't used to eating under anyone's watchful eyes, let alone those of a man like Brice Carlin, whose gaze was sharp and critical.

Still, she ate. Hunger could overcome dozens of inhibitions, she decided. Not that she tasted all she ate. But the juice was just smooth enough, the eggs just soft enough, the toast just crisp enough…which raised an immediate question.

"How did you make the toast?"

"Under the broiler."

She'd tried that once when her toaster had been on the blink. The toast had burned. Apparently Brice had the knack she didn't.

"Did you make the jam?" she asked. It was strawberry, and delicious.

He shook his head. And sat. He had one long leg loosely folded over the other, his elbows on the arms of the chair, his fingers laced. He would have looked perfectly relaxed had not his mouth been so firmly set. And his eyes didn't let up on her for a minute.

By the time she'd finished a little more than half of what he'd served, she set down her fork and frowned at Brice. "What are you staring at?"

He replied with a soft, swift intake of breath, as

though she'd brought him out of a trance. Raising both brows, he shrugged.

"You've done it before," she said. "I feel like I'm on display."

"You are."

"Why?"

He wasn't about to say that she fascinated him, because he didn't want to admit it to himself, much less to her. But there was something about her looks that made him want to look again, and the oddness of that commanded his thought.

She was skinny. Her skin was pale, her eyes shadowed. Her hair was too long, too curly, too dull. So what was he looking at?

He was looking at the smoothness of her pale skin, the dark amber of her shadowed eyes. He was looking at the way one of those too-long curls was caught between the collar of his shirt and her neck, and he was thinking that it was a shade lighter than some, a shade darker than others of those curls, and that if she were in good health it would probably shine. He was also looking at the way his shirt fell over her shoulders, making them look delicate, and the way her breasts made themselves known beneath the slope of soft fabric in front. He was thinking that there was something secretly seductive about the woman—either that or he'd gone soft in the brain.

Sure it was the latter, he snapped himself out of his thoughts and put on a hard face. "You're on display because you're the only woman around."

"If there were others, would they be on display, too?"

"That'd depend. I'm a one-woman man."

"So you'd pick the one who irked you most and focus your stare on her?"

"Probably."

Pushing the tray aside, she slid lower on the pillows. "Has it ever occurred to you that staring that way is unsettling?"

"Uh-huh."

"And that it's impolite?"

"The only people who think that are the ones who are unsettled, and they're only unsettled if they have something to hide."

Turning onto her side, she tugged up the quilt. "A very pointed statement."

"If you take it that way."

"You knew I would. But I'm really not up for it just yet." She closed her eyes. "Maybe later."

Later, though, she slept. With a little food in her stomach to quell her hunger, and regular doses of penicillin and aspirin to work on her illness, she slept deeply.

Shortly after dusk, when the room was cast in darkness, Brice bundled her up and carried her downstairs. She awoke briefly during the trip.

"The bedroom's too cold without heat," he explained in response to her look of confusion. "You'll be better off by the fire until the power comes back on."

She didn't argue, and the minute they reached the living room she knew he was right. The warmth in the air was a stark contrast to the chill upstairs. And then he made her so comfortable on cushions on the floor, and wrapped the quilt so snugly around her that the most natural thing was to close her eyes and go back to sleep.

When next she awoke, the room was darker. She coughed and blearily looked around. The first thing she noticed was that the fire had burned down, the second was that Brice was asleep beside her. Easing out of the quilt, she took several logs from the wood box and placed them over the red-hot embers. They began to smolder, then flame. Returning to the quilt, she tucked herself under it, closed her eyes and willed herself back to sleep. But the chill she'd felt when she'd left the quilt remained with her, and the slight activity of adding logs to the fire had woken her completely.

Lacking anything better to do, she turned her head and studied Brice. He lay on his side facing her. A thick afghan covered him to his ribs; a turtleneck sweater covered the rest. His arms were crossed in front of him, one hand braced on the rug, the other splayed loosely on the opposite shoulder.

She looked at those splayed fingers. Though they were long and lean, there was no delicacy to them, nothing to suggest that he was an artist, or as the case would be, a surgeon. For the first time it struck her that she had no idea what his specialty was.

Not that it mattered.

But she was curious.

Eyes creeping to his face, she studied it for the softening that sleep should have brought. There was little. His jaw was as firm, his mouth as straight, the small line between his brows as marked. In fact, the sole softening came from the fact that his eyes—eyes that could pierce so easily—were closed. Aside from that, he seemed on call.

Hit suddenly by a cough, Karen turned her head away. When she turned back, his eyes were open. Other than tugging the quilt higher, she didn't move. Brice looked at her. She looked right back.

"Have you been up long?" he asked. His voice was thicker, not quite as awake as his eyes.

She shook her head.

He glanced at the fire, saw that she'd added logs. "How do you feel?"

"Better."

"In what way?"

"It doesn't hurt so much when I cough."

"That's good."

During the ensuing silence, it struck Karen that he wasn't a bad-looking man at all. His hair was mussed. He didn't look as stiff. And he wasn't looming over her.

"Are you cold?" he asked.

"I'm okay."

"Are you *cold*?"

"A little."

He sat up, then knelt forward and added another log to those Karen had already fed the fire. She was surprised to see him wearing sweatpants, far softer than the corduroy jeans he'd worn up to then. He hadn't struck her as the soft type. Not that she'd pictured him wearing cords to bed. She hadn't pictured him going to bed at all. Not that he was in bed now. But still. Sweatpants. They looked well worn and fell familiarly over his flanks to outline narrow hips, leanly muscled thighs and a tight butt.

Shocked by her own unexpected analysis, she squeezed her eyes shut. Lying on her side that way, she heard the swish of the afghan as Brice got up, the dull pad of his feet as he left the room. When he returned with several more blankets, she couldn't resist opening her eyes.

"Can you get up?" he asked quietly. "Take the quilt with you."

She managed to stand and move aside while he spread one of the blankets over the cushions. He motioned for her to lie down again, but when she'd settled as she'd been before with her feet closest to the flames, he leaned over and turned her, pillow and all, so that she lay on her side, parallel to the hearth.

"Now I'm hogging the warmth," she protested as he dropped another blanket over her.

"I have more of my own than you do," he stated in a deep, vibrant voice. Stretching out behind her, he drew the afghan to his chest. "Are you warm enough now?"

"I'm okay."

"Are you *warm* enough?"

"Yes." It wasn't exactly true, but she assumed it

would be soon. Already the heat of the fire was reaching out to her. She closed her eyes and concentrated on that welcome warmth, but her concentration was broken by her awareness of Brice.

And the realization that he looked very good in sweatpants.

Swallowing hard at the inappropriateness of the thought, she tucked her legs up and twined her bare feet in the quilt. A minute later, she shifted again, this time to layer one foot over the other, but when that didn't seem to produce the warmth she needed, she shifted again.

"What are you doing?" Brice asked darkly.

"My feet are cold."

"Rub them together."

She tried that, but for the short time she had the strength to keep it up, it didn't do much good.

"Still cold?" he asked.

"Yes."

With a sigh, he moved and before Karen could anticipate his intent, he had joined her under the quilt. "Put your feet between my legs," he instructed.

"Uh, I don't think—"

"Between my legs," he repeated less patiently.

Seconds later, her feet were sandwiched between his calves.

"Better?"

"This is really not—"

"*Better?*"

"Yes."

"Good."

Karen had to admit that it was good. Not only were her feet beginning to thaw, but the rest of her was likewise benefiting from Brice's body heat. As though hearing her thoughts, he wrapped an arm around her waist and pulled her closer.

She stiffened. "Brice?"

"Mmmm?" The hum was muffled by her hair.

She tried to put distance between them, but his arm prevented the movement. "Let me go, Brice," she whispered.

But he wasn't about to. He was oddly comfortable. Without pausing to analyze that comfort, he said, "I won't hurt you. Given that there's no heat and that the fire didn't do the trick, this is the only way I know of to warm you up."

"I'm really *okay*," she said, clutching at his forearm much as she'd done the day before in the car, with similar results. That forearm was made of steel and it wasn't moving.

"Don't fight it, Karen."

"This is unnecessary," she whispered, then began to cough. He brought an arm up between her breasts to support her during the wracking hacks and left it there, hand splayed over her collar bone even after she'd quieted.

And she did quiet. Completely. Her slender body was rigid in his arms.

"Relax," he ordered in a whisper.

She didn't respond in any way.

"Karen?"

"What?"

"I want you to relax."

"I can't."

"I said I wouldn't hurt you."

"I know."

"Then what's the problem?"

"This is very awkward."

"Only because you're so damned stiff. If you'd let go a little, let your body relax back against mine, you'd be fine."

"I was fine before."

"You were cold. Now relax."

She tried, really she did. But the heat emanating from Brice was oddly electric. It sent little tingles up and down the line where his body touched hers. She found it far more unsettling than his stare had ever been.

She tried to wiggle away to sever that bodily contact and ease the tingles, but Brice wasn't having it. "Lie still."

"I can't."

"Why not?"

"I don't know. Maybe you put something in my medicine."

"I did not." He shifted a bit, nestling her more comfortably in his arms.

"Brice," she protested.

"Take a deep breath and let it out very slowly."

She took a deep breath and began to cough. "I'm not good at this," she whispered.

"At what?"

Her whisper grew more frantic. "Touching. I'm not a toucher. I've never slept with a man in my life."

He took a clipped breath. "You're a virgin?"

"I didn't say that. I said I've never slept with a man."

He sighed. "Well, I can understand it. You don't have an awful lot for a man to cuddle up to." When she made a spasmodic move to escape, he held her close and growled, "Stay put."

She did, but she was more tense than ever, because unbidden images were flitting through her mind—images of Brice embracing her in another context, rising over her, possessing her. They were sexual images. She didn't know where they'd come from, only knew that they were wrong. Still they came with startling intensity and persistence. In their shadow, she realized that between the storm and her illness, she was more vulnerable than she'd ever been in her life.

Brice was thinking many of the same things, most notably that if he wanted revenge it was his. Karen couldn't escape him. He could turn her, twist her, terrify her to his heart's content.

If only he were a cruel man.

He'd been accused in his day of being sullen, strange, curt, cold and arrogant, but never cruel. Some of the comments he'd made to Karen had probably come as close to cruel as he'd ever come, but each time he felt badly. As he did now.

She wasn't all *that* scrawny. She had curves in the right places. He could feel those that were cradled against his hips and those that his forearm brushed.

He could also feel her fear, and he wondered about it. He wondered why she didn't like touching, why she'd never spent the night with a man, why she'd never married.

But his wondering took a back seat to her fear.

Loosening his arms, he put the space of several inches between their bodies. "Turn around, Karen," he instructed, but gently.

She didn't move at first.

"Karen."

She turned. His face lay half in her shadow, but that half that was lit by the fire seemed less harsh than usual.

"I won't hurt you," he said quietly. "I told you that at the start, and I've told you several times since, but still you're scared. Why?"

Her answer came in a broken whisper. "I haven't ever felt as helpless as this before. I don't like feeling helpless."

"No one does."

"Some people tolerate it better than others, especially if they...if they..."

"If they what?"

"If they have someone to lean on. Someone to trust."

"And you don't trust me."

She hesitated, then said, "I don't know you."

"But you know my grandmother. You trust her. Don't I stand to inherit some of that trust?"

Karen closed her eyes. She was feeling confused, increasingly weak and tired. "I don't know."

"Okay. Look at it this way. We've been stuck here together now for better than a day. In that time, have I done anything you'd consider untrustworthy?"

"Only…only…"

"Taking you in my arms a little while ago? Karen, I was trying to *warm* you. It's freezing outside, there's no heat inside, and you're sick."

"I know," she wailed softly.

"So why was what I did so bad?"

"It wasn't, I guess."

"Then why were you trembling?"

"I don't know!"

He let out a frustrated breath. "Well, I don't, either."

The fire snapped and sizzled then quieted, and for what seemed an eternity, silence yawned in the darkness between them. But his words echoed and lingered in Karen's mind, bringing her an odd comfort. Knowing that he didn't have all the answers made him seem a bit less powerful, which in turn made her feel a bit less helpless.

Without deliberate intent, she began to relax. She also began to feel sleepy, but then suddenly it seemed important that she tell him something.

"Brice?" she whispered, rushing on before he could answer, "I didn't mean to hurt Rowena. It was so dark that night. I honestly didn't see her. If I could take back what happened, I'd do it in a minute. In a minute. You have no idea—" Her voice cracked. She stopped. When Brice said nothing, she turned over, closed her eyes and prayed that he'd believe her.

For some reason, that mattered to her very much.

4

Karen slept undisturbed until dawn's first light slipped through the living room drapes. She stirred groggily and coughed, then snuggled more neatly into the warmth that framed her back. After a minute she half opened one eye to focus blearily on the fire that was blazing healthily before her. After another minute she opened both eyes to an understanding of the warmth behind.

"Don't," came Brice's deep order. It was rough with sleep and accompanied the faint movement of his chin on the top of her head.

She held her breath and whispered, "Don't what?"

"Don't freeze up. I just got back. I'm tired."

"Got back?"

"From the hospital."

Karen's first thought was that she was delirious. But she didn't feel feverishly hot, and though she was still stuffed up, the congestion wasn't as heavy.

Her second thought was that Brice was talking in his sleep, because what he said made no sense. "You weren't at the hospital."

"I was."

But that would have meant she'd been alone. The

thought was strangely disconcerting. "I didn't hear you leave."

"I got an emergency call," he mumbled. "You slept through it."

She couldn't argue with him. How could she possibly know what had happened while she'd slept? Then another thought dawned. If Brice had been to the hospital and back.... "The storm's over?"

"Mm." He yawned. Karen felt it—the expansion of his chest, the slight elongation of his body—along the length of her spine.

She didn't move. It was a minute before she dared speak. "Are the roads cleared?"

"The main ones," he murmured. "Not mine yet. I hitched a ride in a cruiser."

The main roads were all she needed. She could easily make it down the drive. "Then I'll be able to go home."

"No."

"Why not?"

"Ask me later. I'm too tired now."

It had been a long night for Brice. First he'd lain awake looking at Karen's bundled form and wondering why in the devil he couldn't turn his back on her. Then, just when he'd finally fallen asleep, the hospital had called to say that one of his patients had been brought in with burns suffered in a wood stove mishap.

Burns were the pits. Pain and scarring. He could never become hardened to that, particularly when the victim was a child.

He hadn't returned home seeking comfort in Karen's arms. He'd barely thought of her while he'd been gone. But when he'd walked in and seen her buried beneath the blankets, he'd suddenly felt chilled. He'd no sooner lain down and drawn her to his body when the chills had disappeared and he'd fallen asleep.

It was only natural that he awaken when she moved. For one thing, the internal alarm that had been honed during his internship days was fine-tuned to pick up the slightest noise—the ring of the telephone, a knock at the door, Karen's cough. For another, Karen wasn't the only one who normally slept alone. She moved; he awoke. But he easily fell back to sleep. Given that he'd been up most of Friday night, and then Saturday night watching Karen and that he'd lost the early hours of Sunday to third-degree burns, he was bushed.

Karen could feel that. What she'd initially heard in his voice was reinforced by the laxness of his body. Oh, his heat was there. It ran from the top of her head, where his chin lay, to her feet, which were somehow wound up in his, and, of course, there was the matter of the arm that lay heavily over her waist.

She wasn't bound to him by force, though, and that made the difference between her wanting to bolt and her pausing to consider the positive aspects of her position.

Aside from her face, which was exposed to the air, she was toasty. The quilts and Brice's body heat did that.

She was also surprisingly comfortable. Brice's body was large; she wouldn't have expected it to conform snugly to hers, but it did. With her head on a pillow, her side on cushions and her back supported by his front, she was feeling no pain.

Moreover, she felt unexpectedly safe. Protected. Sheltered. He had a way of doing that to her. It was an illusion, she knew, but still she had no desire to move.

She wasn't sure what Brice thought of the last words she'd whispered to him the night before. She wasn't sure whether he'd even heard them; he'd made no response. But she'd said them, and still he offered his warmth. That had to mean something.

On a note of hope, she fell back to sleep.

Without quite understanding how it happened, she slept through most of the day. It seemed that with the edge of pneumonia eased by penicillin, the exhaustion that had tailed her for far longer than three weeks was taking its due. When she awoke, it was but briefly. Brice brought her light meals—eggs, soup, pudding, cocoa—but she had trouble eating much. Her stomach seemed to have shrunk. She was frighteningly weak. As soon as he freed her of the small tray across her lap, she slid down to the pillow and fell back to sleep.

At some point during the afternoon, the electricity returned, but she remained before the fire on the living room sofa, wrapped in blankets. Each time she stirred, she made feeble sounds about needing to go home, but Brice repeatedly put her off. It wasn't until

early evening that she mustered the strength to confront him.

She'd been lying alone for a while when that
strength hit. Or maybe it was panic that hit. She was
thinking of all she wasn't accomplishing, and the psychological restlessness had built and built until it
reached fever pitch. So she wrapped herself in a blanket and went in search of Brice.

Finding him took some doing. He was in neither
of the rooms on the other side of the hall. The kitchen
and pantry were likewise empty. She was wondering
if she had the strength to take her search up the stairs,
when her eye fell on the entry to what she'd assumed
to be a storage room. Closer inspection showed it to
be the entry to a whole other wing of the house.

Brice was in a room off the paneled hall that looked
to be his private den. The walls were lined from ceiling to floor with dark maple bookshelves, which were
in turn lined with books. What little open wall space
there was was filled with small and varied works of
art, rather than diplomas. An Oriental rug overspread
the floor, providing a cushion for an aged leather sofa
and a sturdy oak desk.

Brice had his heels on the desk, ankles crossed. He
was leaning back in the chair with his fingers laced
on his middle, and though his gaze met hers the minute she appeared at the door, he said nothing.

If Karen had worried about facing him in a second-
floor bedroom, her fears were doubled here. She had
the distinct feeling that she had fallen upon sacred
ground. The room was Brice. It was serious and com-

plex, dark and silent. She sensed that this was where he spent a good deal of his free time and that if she were to examine the books packed on the shelves she'd find them as well worn and diverse as they were revealing. In that sense, the room was incredibly intimate.

For a fleeting instant she recalled the way Brice's body had warmed hers during the night. Then the instant passed, leaving tingles in its wake.

Clearing her throat, she ran an eye around the room and said in a quietly sincere, sandy voice, "I'm impressed."

Brice had recalled that warming, too. He'd thought about it a lot since it had happened, had tried to make sense of it. But he couldn't. Now he looked at Karen and wondered about the satisfaction he'd felt when he'd held her in his arms.

In answer to both her comment and his thoughts, he gave a slow, begrudging shrug.

"Have you read them all?" she asked.

"Most."

"When do you read?"

"Evenings. Weekends."

"You have the time?"

"Of course."

She was envious. She was also puzzled. "I wouldn't have thought it—your being a doctor and all."

"Doctors don't work round the clock. They have lives like everyone else."

"But there are so many books up there." She

scanned the shelves. "So many hours of involvement." Her gaze met his. "Were you always an avid reader?"

He hesitated. He wasn't used to being questioned about himself. The town knew him as a fine doctor who was intensely private. He was comfortable with the combination. Those few people who had tried to penetrate the private man behind the stethoscope had been quickly, even rudely put off. They hadn't tried again.

He wasn't quite sure what category to put Karen in. She wasn't a townsperson. Nor, at that moment, was she a patient. He would have called her a friend of Rowena's if the circumstances of that friendship weren't so odd, and on that score he had his own questions to ask. Karen wasn't the only one who was curious.

But she'd asked first. And he had nothing to lose by answering. "I used to read a lot as a kid. When I was in med school, I barely had time to breathe, much less read."

Karen tried to picture a younger Brice Carlin, sweeping up and down the corridors of a hospital in the crisp white garb of an intern. It was hard to imagine him in as busy a setting. He seemed so dark, so quiet, so solitary. Yes, the phone rang on occasion, and there had been the trip to the hospital he'd made early that morning, but she couldn't picture him as part of a team, dealing with other doctors, nurses and technicians, much less patients and their families.

She could picture him studying, though, leaning

over a deskful of books with his dark hair falling on his brow and his eyes unwavering on the page. Then she pictured herself studying, leaning over a deskful of books with her eyes unwavering on the page and she was hit by the edginess that had brought her in search of her host.

Drawing herself as straight as she could, she looked him in the eye and said in her firmest voice, "I have to leave, Brice. I appreciate all you've done for me, but I can't stay any longer." The words tumbled out with increasing speed. "The roads are passable. Your driveway's been plowed. There has to be someone I can call to take a look at my car." Feeling winded, she sucked in her lower lip, then watched in dismay as, without taking his eyes from hers, Brice slowly but firmly shook his head. Somewhere in the back of her mind, she'd expected it, but that didn't make it any easier to take. She wasn't feeling up to par. She didn't really want to fight him.

"Why not?" she asked with caution.

He unlaced his hands enough to run one flat palm over his chest. He was wearing another sweater—this one with a cable that ran up the left front—and the way his hand glided over it suggested it was made of cashmere. Karen wished he were an iota as soft as the fabric.

He wasn't.

"For one thing," he began with a bluntness bordering on the blasé, "no one is going to look at your car tonight. The people who could fix it are the same ones who have been digging this town out of the snow for the past twenty-four hours. If I were to call, they'd laugh—*if* they were home, which I doubt they are—but I wouldn't think of calling.''

''I'll call.''

''Same difference. Those guys are exhausted. Their work is far from done.''

''A dead battery isn't part of their work?''

''Not this weekend. There's fifteen inches of snow out there, more where it's drifted. That's a hell of a lot to shovel.''

''I'm just asking for a jump start. I'd think that would be a break for them.''

''Think again. A break is being indoors, drinking hot coffee laced with something strong enough to preserve the heat. Your car is under the same fifteen inches of snow as the road. It has to be shoveled out before the hood can even be raised. And besides, how do you know a jump start is all it needs? From the looks of that car, the battery may be hopeless. *If* the problem is with the battery. Are you sure it is?''

She was beginning to feel a little shaky. ''No.''

''If it's not the battery, the car will have to be towed, and believe me, you'll have trouble finding a tow truck that isn't plowing. And even if you get someone to tow you to a station,'' he went on in that same deep, infuriatingly placid voice, ''it'll be at least another day or two before someone will take a look at the car. The high school kid who pumps gas—if he's there at all in this weather—won't know what to do with a car that doesn't start.''

Karen wanted to cry. She was as frustrated by the

situation as she was annoyed by Brice's blunt summarization. If he'd sounded at all smug she'd probably have hurled a book at him. But he hadn't sounded smug, just hard, and she doubted she'd have been able to hurl a book far. Feeling a dire need to sit, she stumbled to the sofa.

"How about a cab or a bus?" she asked as she sank gratefully into the pliant leather folds. She tucked up her knees and rewrapped the blanket so that all of her was covered.

Brice shrugged a single brow. "I doubt you'll get either." He had his fingers laced again and was studying her more intently. "Why the rush? Most of the world looks outside, sees the snow and rejoices at an unexpected holiday. If you can't go anywhere, you can't go anywhere. There's no sense beating your head against a brick wall."

"But is it a brick wall? That's what I need to know. If there's some way for me to get home, I'd like to take it."

"What's so special at home? Do you have a cat to feed?"

"I have work to do."

"And you're well enough to do it?"

She hugged her knees tight. "You don't understand. I *have* to do it. Classes may be canceled for a day or two—" her eyes widened in sudden alarm and she came forward "—I don't even know if they will be. For all I know, the storm was *nothing* in Syracuse!"

"It was worse."

She let out a breath. "Thank goodness." When Brice snorted, she added a hasty, "I don't mean to sound callous. But if it was business as usual, I'd be in hot water." Her brows met in a look of panic. "As it is, I'll probably lose my job."

"You won't lose your job," Brice said. "I talked with the owner of the Pepper Mill and explained that you were sick. He suggested you take off until after vacation."

Karen went very still. "Excuse me?"

"I talked with Jason Grant. You were supposed to work last night, weren't you?"

She didn't answer his question but sank weakly back into the sofa. "I don't believe you called Jason. I don't believe you said I wouldn't be in until after vacation." Silently she cursed herself for having been out of it for the past forty-eight hours. Less silently she cursed Brice for having taken over her life. "Damn it, you shouldn't have done that. You had no right. I have to work! I need the money!"

Brice had expected her anger. He supposed, when he thought about it, that he'd have been disappointed if she'd sat back and let him take over without a peep. If she'd done that, he'd have guessed she'd accept whatever charity he was willing to offer.

He was a generous man. Over the course of a year, he gave as much to charity as many people made for a living. But he picked and chose his causes, and a woman had never been one of them.

He'd already decided that Karen was independent, and while her occasional bullheadedness riled him, he

was oddly assured by her show of pride now. It said
that she wouldn't take advantage of him. Perversely,
her self-sufficiency made it all that much more rewarding for him to do for her. Yes, he was pleased
that he'd spoken with Jason Grant. He was pleased
that he'd bought a little rest time for Karen. Given
the condition she'd been in when he'd found her in
the snow, she needed it.

All he had to do was to convince *her* of that.

Removing his feet from the desk, he crossed an
ankle over his knee. "You won't be able to work at
all unless you take care of yourself. You've been very
sick and you're a long way from cured. How do you
feel now?"

"Fine," she said on a single breath of boldness.

"How?" he repeated.

The boldness faded. "Okay."

"Is that why you dragged yourself away from the
door and collapsed on the sofa?"

"I didn't drag and I didn't collapse."

He would have laughed at her disgruntled expression if he'd been the laughing type, but he wasn't.
"Sure looked it to me."

"You saw what you wanted to see," she argued.
She was feeling contrary, but her voice was weak-
ening. "You're a doctor. If people were well all the
time, you'd be out of business."

The small muscle at Brice's temple twitched.
"That was a stupid thing to say."

She surprised him by looking contrite. "I think it
came out wrong. What I meant was that you're at-

tuned to seeing illness, therefore it's possible you see illness where there really is none."

"Are you saying you're perfectly all right now? That you're well? Feeling one-hundred percent?"

"No."

"You do admit that there's still something a little foreign running around in your system?"

She hesitated, then murmured a reluctant, "Yes."

"If that's true, should you be waitressing?" His eyes sharpened on her. "Don't think of yourself, Karen. Think of the people you'd be waiting on. If you were working in an accounting office, or sitting behind a computer all day, it'd be one thing for you to work through a cold—not that I'd recommend it, but that would be different from being sick and waitressing. You handle the food people eat."

"I know," she said. She hated him for being so sensible.

"And you still think you should be working?"

"No..." she admitted, and took in a breath to argue, only to be beaten to it by Brice.

"But you need the money."

She let out the breath. "Yes." She rested her head against the sofa and eyed the ceiling. Brice's voice came to her more gently then.

"How do you feel now?"

"Discouraged."

"Physically, how do you feel? I want to know where we stand for treatment."

She closed her eyes and tried to separate psychological edginess from the purely physical symptoms.

"I feel tired," she said in a small voice. "I don't hurt as much. I'm not swinging hot to cold. But my legs don't seem to want to carry me far. I feel—" she searched for another word, but the first one she'd used seemed to sum it all up "—tired."

"You need rest."

"I've *had* rest. I've done little more than sleep for the past forty-eight hours."

"That sleep was for the infection. The sleep you need now is for you, and above and beyond that you need rest. There's a difference."

She heard what he said, understood what he meant, but the facts didn't change. "I don't have the time."

"Make the time."

"That's easier said than done," she wailed softly. "I agree that I should take time off from the Pepper Mill, but I still have papers and midterms, and Professor McGuire will be expecting me in his office tomorrow afternoon. I have to get back to Syracuse."

There was a pregnant silence. Karen saw something in Brice's eyes that she didn't like. Her pulse tripped.

"I spoke to McGuire," he told her.

"Oh, no." She squeezed her eyes shut. "I enjoyed that job, Brice. Professor McGuire was as interesting as his work."

"Why the past tense?"

She opened her eyes. "Because he has deadlines to meet and there are *dozens* of students willing to work for him. I'm sure he's hired someone else by now."

"He hasn't."

"How do you know?" she asked indignantly.

"I know. You still have the job."

Her indignation vanished. "I do?" When he nodded, she rushed on. "But he needs the work done."

"In time. He'll be away over vacation, anyway. Skiing in the Alps."

She stared, then murmured, "Oh."

"He said he'll meet with you when classes reconvene."

Turning sideways, Karen closed her eyes.

"Aren't you pleased?" Brice asked. He was rather proud of himself for having arranged things so well. "You have your job and a vacation." She remained still. "Karen?"

She sighed, looked at him, then said in a meek voice, "Thank you."

For the first time, Brice was roused from his pose of total control. Uncrossing his legs, he set his forearms on the desk. "I had better thanks from the kid I diagnosed as having chicken pox on the day before he was to leave for Disney World. But that's okay. I wasn't looking for your thanks. I was looking to buy you a breather from the hell of a schedule you've got. When was the last time you had a vacation?"

"I don't know."

"*When*?"

"I can't remember."

"What do you *do* with yourself?"

"I work."

"All the time? You're not *that* hard up for money, are you?"

She was resting her head on the soft leather, feeling very tired again. Perhaps for that reason, her defenses were down. The pride that might have kept her silent wasn't on guard. In a voice that was less nasal than it had been, but still hoarse and very soft, she said, "The earliest memories I have are of tension in my family. I couldn't have been more than three or four years old, but I remember it. My dad couldn't hold down a job. My mom never criticized him for it, but there was constant worry about how she was going to pay the bills."

Brice didn't want to hear her story, didn't want to feel for her. He opened his mouth to tell her to stop, then closed it again. He wanted to hear every word. He had to know more. He told himself it was the doctor in him needing a history, which was far easier to swallow than the idea that the man in him was the one in need.

So he didn't say a word. And Karen, seeming tired and weak but determined to talk, went on.

"My father had been in construction and had planned to start his own company. Then there was an accident. His legs were crushed under a wall of concrete. The doctors managed to rebuild them, but by the time that was done, whatever money he'd saved had gone for medical bills. There was a small settlement from a lawsuit, but he went through that almost as quickly, because by that time he was addicted to painkillers and they cost a bundle."

"Did your mother work?"

"She took in other children and called it babysitting, though she was really running a daycare center from our house. I thought it was great. I didn't have any brothers or sisters, and there were suddenly lots of kids around. Then the state got fussy about licensing. Mom couldn't get a license because we didn't have the money to make the repairs that would have been required. So she was reduced to really doing babysitting—for no more than one or two kids at a time—and the money that brought in wasn't enough to support the three of us. When I started school, she went to work as a secretary in a small law office. The pay helped, but it was never spectacular. She could type. She couldn't take dictation because she didn't know shorthand, and she didn't have the time or money to go to school for it."

Karen recalled her mother's frustration. Even at nine, ten, eleven years of age she could understand what it meant to want to earn a living and not be able to.

"Was your dad at home for you after school?" Brice asked.

"Sometimes."

"Was he...kind to you?"

That brought a spark. Her head came up a fraction, eyes focusing more clearly on Brice. "He was never a cruel man. He was frustrated and unhappy, went from one job to the next in the hope that the newest would be the best, but there was always the physical pain and the need for drugs. He never touched alcohol. He was never violent. But he was totally unreliable. Spaced out. Foggy. A couple of times he fell into a coma. He was rushed to the hospital and the doctors said all the right words about weaning him from the habit, but he signed himself out before it could be done. My mother tried to convince him to enroll in this or that program, but he argued that he couldn't if he wanted to help support his family. So he went from one job to the next. It was a Catch-22.''

She dropped her head back again and fell silent, remembering the nights she'd lain in bed listening to the soft sounds of her mother crying. The woman suffered pain on all sides. Karen had vowed to help wherever she could.

"As soon as I graduated from high school, I went to work full-time.'' She paused, frowned. "I thought I was doing my parents a favor, but sometimes I wonder if my working didn't bring my mother more pain than relief. She wanted me to go to college. She saw women with lucrative careers, and that was what she wanted for me. She was a bright woman, but her only training was as a housewife, and there was no pay for that.'' Again Karen paused. Again she frowned. "It was a Catch-22 for me, too. Mom wanted me to stop working and go to college for the education that would have guaranteed me a better income, but I didn't have that luxury because we needed the money right then. Dad was in and out of the hospital more often; he had kidney problems and liver problems. The bills kept coming in.''

She closed her eyes and sank lower into her blanket while Brice watched tiny lines of pain etch her brow. His heart went out to her, while the cynic in him had a fleeting moment's rise. If she'd set out to spin a heart-wrenching tale, she'd succeeded well.

Then he remembered how she'd begun crying on the first day he'd brought her to his house, how she'd withdrawn into herself, seeming mortified. Though there was no mortification now, there was the same kind of pained withdrawal, the same kind of introversion. Now, as then, she refused to look at him.

Rising from his chair, he tucked his hands deep in the pockets of his cords and walked slowly, almost idly around the desk. He stopped several feet from the sofa when she began to speak again. She was frowning at her thumb, picking its nail.

"When I was nineteen, I met a man. Boy—man— he was twenty-three. He was an artist, or thought himself one, though to this day he hasn't hit the big time. I was doing odd jobs—typing, filing, telephoning— for the curator of a small museum in New Haven, not far from where we lived. I loved art."

Her expression softened, though she didn't look up. "I met Tim at the museum and I loved him, too. He was everything I'd never known—carefree, lighthearted, fun-loving. I felt like a different person when I was with him." She frowned at her hand. "But I was living a dual life—working hard, counting my pennies, giving every spare cent to my parents, then going off with Tim for an afternoon picnic or an evening with his friends or a weekend on a secluded beach where he was supposed to be inspired."

"Was he?"

She gave a sad little laugh. "Not usually. We just...had...fun."

Brice felt a vague tightening around his heart. It wasn't that he was jealous of the man, because he had no claim on Karen, but there was something about that soft look on her face, something about the sadness in her laughter and the fact that it had been the first laughter of any kind that he'd heard pass her lips, that touched him deeply. Her skin was smooth, her face lined by nothing but fatigue and the occasional frown. He'd never seen her smile. It was a shame.

"What happened to him?"

She'd been thinking back to those fun times, remembering how nice it had been to forget her worries, if only for a short time. Brice's question brought her back to the present with a start. "Tim? Uh, we parted ways."

Brice had never been a gossip-monger, but he couldn't believe she'd leave him high and dry that way. So he asked, "Why?"

She shrugged. "I wasn't what he thought."

"What do you mean?"

"He thought I had money."

For a minute there was silence. Then Brice said, "Go on."

Head back against the sofa, she closed her eyes. Her voice was weary. "He was looking for someone to bankroll his career. Someone to support him while he sketched. Somehow he got the impression that I was wealthy. Maybe it was the way I dressed. I had an eye for style and could take a nothing piece of clothing and wrap it or knot it or belt it into something interesting. Or maybe it was the way I walked or talked. He said I sounded aristocratic. Cultured. He assumed there was money attached. I never took him home with me. I didn't want to blur the lines between my two worlds. Besides, my parents would have hated him on sight.''

"So how did he find out?''

"I think,'' she said more slowly, "that he was beginning to ask himself whether I was worth the investment of his energy, and the only way he could know that was to see how I lived.'' She took a stuffy breath. "He found out, all right. The apartment we lived in was nice enough, but it was an apartment and it was small and it wasn't in the greatest of neighborhoods.'' Still, she remembered that apartment with fondness, because it was the place she'd called home for twenty-three years. Tim had felt no fondness for it at all. "We broke up soon after that.''

Brice felt a flare of anger—at both Karen and her beau—and when he was angry, he was blunt. "How could you have fallen for him?''

Hurt, she looked up. "I didn't know what he was after.''

"It should have been obvious. Was he that great an actor that he could pretend feelings he didn't have?''

Karen was the one to be angry then. Her anger gave her the strength to sit straight. "I wasn't blind or dumb, Brice. Tim wasn't pretending. He really did like me. He just wanted more.'' Shifting the blankets, she stood. "He was totally up-front about things when we broke up. I'm not sure that made it any easier for me, but when a guy is blunt like that about something so basic, what can you say?" She turned and moved toward one of the book-lined walls. "My heart wasn't broken, so I couldn't have been that desperately in love, either. But I was disillusioned. I think I'd have preferred to break up for any other reason than that."

Sighing, she absently fingered the camera that lay on one of the shelves. "The only thing was, the experience burned me a little. So there weren't any other men like Tim, and I kept on working. I did love my work. I loved—still do love—sitting in a room where I'm surrounded by fine pieces of art."

Brice could believe that about her. She looked the type. Rowena certainly was the type. For that matter, *he* was the type. He appreciated solitude and silence, and he appreciated artistic skill. "Do you draw or paint?"

"No. I can't do either. That's why I'm in art history instead of fine arts."

But that was getting ahead of her story, and Brice wanted to hear the whole thing. So, standing across from her with his hands in his pockets, he asked, "What finally happened to your parents?"

Tugging the blanket around her shoulder, she stared unseeingly at the books on the shelves. She was tired, but something inside made her speak. "My dad died when I was twenty-one. He left lots of bills. Mom and I were chipping away at them—doing pretty well, actually—when she got sick. I was twenty-three when she died. It was two more years before I'd paid off the last of the bills.''

''Was that when you decided to go back to school?''

She gave a small headshake. ''I had decided that years ago. It was just a question of when I could swing it. After the bills were paid, I started building a kitty so I could study full-time.'' She lowered her chin to her chest. ''Then I hit Rowena. You know the rest.''

Brice didn't know the rest, but he could piece it together. She'd needed that kitty to pay her lawyer, and by the time she'd finished, she was back to square one. ''So you put togther an impossible program for yourself,'' he said darkly. He wasn't sure who most annoyed him at that moment—Karen for speeding down a dark country road, Rowena for bicycling without reflectors, fate for putting the two women at the same spot at the same time, or himself for hurting for them both. ''You're pushing yourself at a pace that would try even the hardiest of people.''

She turned a pleading look his way. ''I have no choice. Don't you see? I've been caught in the same bind for so long that the only way I can escape it is to make it through these four years. Once they're done, I'll be able to breathe free.''

''Because you'll be earning good money?''

He didn't understand. That hurt. ''It's not only the money,'' she cried. ''If it were, I'd be after a degree in business, rather than one in art history.'' Averting her gaze, she made for the door, but Brice was suddenly before her, blocking her escape.

"What is it, then?"

She looked into his eyes. They were as dark as ever, but involved. They challenged her. "It's getting out from under the heap. Being on top. Calling the shots, rather than having the shots call me. I don't need millions to live on. My tastes aren't extravagant. All I want is to be able to go to bed at night knowing that I've paid my bills. Is that too much to ask?"

Her gaze dropped to his mouth as she waited for him to respond. His lips were firm, boldly cut, masculine. They pressed together and she felt it. She raised her eyes in a hurry and they collided with his. They were dark. Sensual. They stunned her.

"Rowena was worried about you," he said distractedly as he tried to decide whether Karen's eyes were amber or brown.

"About me?"

"She called to tell me that your car was still in the lot. She wanted me to call the police."

Charcoal gray, Karen decided, and slightly lighter in the center. His eyes were captivating. "Did you tell her I was here?"

"Uh-huh. She was relieved. She knew you were sick."

"She shouldn't have worried."

His gaze fell to her mouth. "She likes you."

"I like her, too."

"Is that why you visit her twice a week?"

"That's…one of the reasons," Karen said, but her

voice was shaky. She had the strangest urge to touch
Brice's face, the strangest urge to see what that dark
shadow on his jaw felt like. It was taking all her
strength not to give in to those strangest of urges, and
she didn't have much strength to begin with. "I
think...I'd better sit down," she whispered.

"Tell me the other reasons," Brice said thickly. He
was fascinated by the small blush that lit her cheeks.
It was a world away from the fever touch he'd seen
before.

She could have moved, but she didn't. Her eyes
were locked with his, her voice wispy. "Please...I'd
like to sit."

He slid his hands down her arms as they were outlined under the blanket, but the small support that
movement gave was offset by the greater weakness
his touch inspired. Karen wasn't so faint or ill or out
of practice that she didn't recognize the weakness for
desire. She was attracted to Brice. That frightened her.

"What are the other reasons you visit Rowena?"
he asked. It wasn't weakness he was feeling but the
opposite, and in a totally unexpected part of his body.
Just then he wanted to hold Karen close. But he
couldn't. He wasn't supposed to like her.

"We have fun together," Karen murmured.

"You read to her."

"We both like that."

"But twice a week—that's three hours of driving."

"I don't mind."

"I'd think you wouldn't have the time," he said.
He was thinking that he wanted to kiss her.

"I make the time."

He couldn't kiss her. "Gas costs."

"I pay gladly."

He couldn't like her. His fascination had to stop. "Is it guilt?"

She stiffened, then felt a wave of weakness that had nothing to do with desire. "No."

The soft infusion of warmth had washed from her face. Brice was relieved. He didn't want her looking kissable. "Guilt would be the normal thing to feel."

Karen knew that a special moment had passed and didn't understand what had happened. In addition to weak, she felt raw. Her response to Brice was defensive. "It started out as that, but it isn't now."

"You don't feel *any* guilt?"

"I didn't say that."

"Do you feel it?"

"Yes. I live with it all the time. I blame myself for not having somehow seen Rowena that night. I blame myself for not having concentrated more closely on the road that night, for not having cleaned my headlights, for not having driven way over on the right-hand shoulder of the road. I feel guilt. But that's not why I visit Rowena."

"Are you admitting that you were to blame that night?"

Tears gathered in her eyes. "No!"

"But you just said—"

"That I blame myself. That's different from admitting I was responsible for the accident." Trembling, she tried to pull back from his grasp, but he wasn't easing up. "I didn't lie during the trial, Brice. You sat there. You heard what I said. I wasn't speeding. I don't drink or do drugs." Her voice was getting more and more hoarse. "I didn't break any law that night, so I fought the charges you brought against me—"

"I didn't—"

"The district attorney did, but you were behind it, and you were wrong. I can understand what you did. She's your grandmother and you love her. But you were wrong. It wasn't fair—" Her voice broke, but she was determined to say it, so she started again, this time sniffling from the tears that were trickling down her cheeks. "It wasn't right that after everything I'd been through I should have been f-further penalized because Rowena and I were on that road together that night." His face was a dark blur through her tears, but she raced on. "If it's some consolation to you, I've suffered anyway. Each time I see her I remember that it was *my* car that put her where she is."

She tipped her face sideways into the blanket at her shoulder and cried softly, wishing Brice would let her go, wishing she could break away, wishing she were anywhere else at that moment. Absurdly, she murmured, "Sh-she's the grandmother I never had. I l-love her, too."

Closing his eyes, Brice brought her into his arms. He didn't care what he was supposed to feel or what he wasn't. She wasn't well. And now she was hurting more.

Cupping her head, he held it to his chest while he

supported her with an arm around her waist. He could feel her body trembling, could hear her soft weeping. He sensed her getting weaker with each passing minute, and lest she fall, he lifted her and carried her to the sofa. Then he sat with her on his lap and shifted the blankets so that he could hold her closer. He stroked her hair, restrained in its barrette. He stroked her slender back, rubbed her neck, her arms. He held her until she'd stopped crying. Then he carried her, sound asleep, to the second floor bedroom he'd come to think of as hers, tucked her into bed and left the room.

5

When Karen awoke, it was morning. Turning over in bed, she slowly opened her eyes to a winter sun whose rays were all the brighter for their own reflection on the snow. The drapes were gilded, the floor bathed in light. It was a cheery welcome to the day and went a long way toward compensating for the face of her watch, which proclaimed the time to be 9:40.

She couldn't believe that she'd slept the night through after having slept away the day before. A little voice told her that Brice had been right, that she was exhausted, that her body not only needed but demanded the rest. She listened to that little voice for as long as it took for the events of the evening before to return. Then she turned over again, bunched the pillow under her head and tried to understand what she felt.

It was a tall order, because Brice was an enigma. She had never pictured herself with the dark, silent type. Tim had been slim and fair. By comparison, physically and otherwise, Brice was more substantial.

What had happened the night before in his den? She'd been talking with him, telling him about her family. He'd been looking interested and very attractive. They'd come to be standing close, and she'd felt warm and excited. She had felt wanted.

Then Brice had gone cold. He'd turned off the appeal by steering the conversation to Rowena and jabbing her with it. Karen felt as though she'd been punished.

Perhaps it was just as well, though. She had no time for a man, especially not now when she was on the verge of solvency. She couldn't be distracted, which was why she had to get back to Syracuse. McGuire and the Pepper Mill could be put off with little more than a loss of wages. But if she didn't write her paper, if she didn't start studying for midterms she'd be up a creek. There were no refunds for failed courses.

Tossing aside the covers, she quickly sat up, then steadied herself with a hand by each hip. She felt strange. Dizzy. But her head was clearer than it had been. She closed her eyes until the dizziness passed. She sniffed several times to find that her stuffiness had eased. She coughed. It was still a heavy cough, but nowhere near as bad as it had been, and it brought no pain. She was definitely on the mend.

Then she lowered her feet to the floor and stood— and quickly sat back down. Her legs felt like rubber. Her entire body felt disjointed.

"All from one weekend's disuse," she murmured, but she knew it wasn't true. The enervation she felt was the result not of disuse but abuse. She'd been driving herself too hard. She'd known it, but she'd had no other choice.

Thanks to Brice, she'd had another choice over the

weekend and she'd taken it—perhaps not willingly, but she'd done it. She'd slept. Rested. Healed. But even if the healing process wasn't done, the weekend was. She had to get going.

More slowly shifting her weight to her feet, she stood. Closely circling the bedposts, she walked to the window.

The scene before her sparkled. Though the snow had been no ally, it was beautiful. Of course, it had something to work with; Brice's land was spectacular. Much of the landscaping was ancient, evident from the incredible size of the pines. The newer plantings weren't as large, but they were full and healthy, and had been craftily sculpted into the land.

The driveway had been plowed. Pressing her nose to the glass, she followed its curve around, past the front door toward the area she assumed to be his office. She couldn't see the entrance, but she could see the small plowed spot where several cars were parked.

Brice was at work.

Curious to get a look at one or two of his patients, she lingered at the window for a minute. But her legs quickly tired, so she sank into the rocker and tried to decide what to do next.

She had to find her clothes, take a cab back to the nursing home, call someone to repair her car and get back to Syracuse. But part of her didn't want to do any of that. Part of her wanted to stay where she was, enjoying the comfort of the house, the warmth of the room, the overall ambiance, cozy and relaxed. Part of

her, she realized with a shock, wanted to stay and be
taken care of by Brice.

That couldn't happen.

So she set her mind to thinking of what *could* happen and when. She had barely reached the point of
wishing for a bath when she heard the sound of footsteps in the hall. Her heart skipped a beat, then sped.
But the footsteps were too light to be Brice's, and
besides, he was working. Eyes on the door, she
watched it open a crack. The small face that peered
through was female and was framed by thin, smooth
blond shoulder-length hair. A slight tapping sound
edged the door open wider. The girl carried Karen's
breakfast tray, but she stood at the door unsurely.

Karen had never seen as delicate-looking a creature. At first glance, she couldn't believe that the girl
could be Brice's maid. At second glance, she realized
that the girl was a woman—probably in her early
twenties. She wore sneakers, a pair of pencil-slim,
worn jeans and a large, heavy Irish knit sweater. And
she was waiting, eyeing Karen nervously, in need of
direction.

Karen made a small beckoning motion with her
hand. That seemed to be what the girl needed, because she promptly cleared the threshold and crossed
to the rocker. She started to lower the tray to Karen's
lap, then drew it back and looked over her shoulder
at the bed.

"It would be more stable there," Karen said gently.

The blond-haired creature quickly looked at her, both eyebrows raised in question.

Karen rephrased the thought. "Whatever's on your tray may spill if I rock by mistake. I think I'd be better in bed." Rising from the chair, she climbed back under the covers and smoothed a section beside her for the tray.

The girl set it down and shyly stepped away, but rather than leaving, she backed toward the foot of the bed. After tucking a lock of gossamer hair behind her ear, she wrapped an arm around the bedpost. She looked at Karen, then the floor, then Karen again. Finally, and with some nervousness, she asked, "How are you feeling?"

They were the first words she'd offered, and Karen instantly knew why. Yes, Brice's maid was young and shy. She was also severely hard of hearing. The heavily nasal quality of her voice—totally different from the nasality of a cold—and her slightly aberrant diction suggested it. With that clue and a single glance, Karen detected a hearing aid in her ear.

"I'm feeling better," she said, noting that the girl's eyes followed her lips. "Thank you." She looked down at the tray. It held a glass of orange juice, a plate filled with scrambled eggs, sausage and potato, two pieces of toast with a dollop of jam, and a mug of hot chocolate. "This looks delicious. I'm hungry."

The girl looked relieved. "Dr. Carlin said to make lots and to be sure you ate it. He said you needed to gain weight." She paused, shy again. "I don't think so. I think you're perfect."

Karen looked up in time to catch a blush on the girl's face. "You're very kind," she said in a tone suggesting she thought of herself as anything but perfect. "What's your name?"

"Meg."

"Mine's Karen."

"I know."

Karen took a drink of juice, found it to be fresh squeezed and took another, longer drink. Her taste buds were responding; it was the first time in weeks that she'd truly savored something.

She looked up to find Meg's eyes large and watchful. Holding up the glass, she asked, "Did you squeeze it yourself?"

Meg nodded, but made no move to leave, which put Karen in a bind. She was ignorant of the protocol involving household help. She wasn't sure whether she was expected to eat, talk or do neither. Somehow saying, "You can go now," didn't seem right at all.

Curiosity was the deciding factor. If Meg worked for Brice, she had to know something about him. So Karen asked, "Have you worked for Dr. Carlin long?"

"Two years."

"How did you meet up with him?"

"He knows my husband's family."

It hadn't occurred to Karen that Meg might be married. She seemed too young, too innocent. But, looking, Karen saw the thin platinum band that circled the ring finger of the girl's left hand. "When?" she asked, tossing her chin toward the ring. Then she looked up, prepared to state the full question if Meg hadn't been able to read her verbal shorthand.

Meg read it. She blushed again and smiled. "Two years ago. I was working in a daycare center in Schenectady when Richie—that's my husband—came to do some work. He's an electrician. He brought me here to live just when Dr. Carlin was needing help. The woman before me had been with him for a long time, but I guess they argued a lot. He finally got tired of the arguments." She looked puzzled. "I don't know what they argued about. I've never found anything to argue about with him. He's a nice, quiet man."

Karen could have argued with that; she'd seen a different side of the man. He could be domineering, sharp, sarcastic. But he seemed to take to the wounded. When she'd been feeling at her worst over the weekend, he'd been gentle. When she'd been upset last night, he'd been gentle. He was apparently gentle with Meg. She guessed that he'd be gentle with his patients.

"What kind of practice does he have?" she asked.

But Meg was worriedly eyeing the tray and didn't hear. "That's your penicillin pill in the little cup. You'd better take it."

If for no other reason than to erase that look of worry, Karen promptly took the pill with a swallow of juice. Then, lifting her fork, she started in on the eggs. The first mouthful went down so pleasantly that she went on to a second, then sampled the sausage and potatoes in turn.

"I hope you know," she paused to say, "that I feel decadent having breakfast in bed. You'd think I was one of the idle rich."

Meg was suspiciously silent. Looking up, Karen saw a face filled with confusion.

"I'm not rich," she assured her. "I'm not usually idle, either."

The confusion remained. "Are you a relative of Dr. Carlin's?"

"No."

"A friend, then?"

Karen considered that. Three days before she'd never have put Brice in the category of friend, but a lot had happened since then. On some level, they remained adversaries. On another level, though, yes, they were friends. At least, she thought that way.

"Actually," she answered on a note of greater sureness, "I'm a friend of Dr. Carlin's grandmother. I was visiting her when I took sick."

Meg nodded her understanding, but she seemed disappointed. Belatedly, it occurred to Karen that Meg had been speculating on the relationship being a romantic one, particularly with Karen wearing what was so obviously Brice's shirt.

"Is Dr. Carlin's grandmother's name Rowena?" she asked.

"Yes."

She grew sheepish. "I wasn't sure if that was his mother or a sister or ex-wife."

Ex-wife. A new thought. Karen wasn't sure she liked it.

"No. Rowena is his grandmother."

"I've taken calls from her sometimes—there's an amplifier of the phone downstairs. Well, they're not really from her but from someone announcing that she's calling. I have orders to put those calls right through to the office." She paused, offered a hesitant half smile. "I've always pictured Rowena Carlin as a rich lady whose personal secretary places the calls. Am I right?"

Karen knew that Rowena had always been a free spirit, that she had always traveled, that she appreciated a fine wine and was sophisticated in her way. In truth, though, Karen had no idea whether Rowena was wealthy. She did know that the calls coming in weren't made by a personal secretary.

What stunned her, though, was that Meg didn't know about Rowena—either that she was Brice's grandmother or that she was confined in a nursing home. Karen couldn't understand the rationale behind it. If Meg had been with him for a week or a month, she could see where something like that might have slipped through. But the girl had been with him for two years. She was shy; perhaps she'd never asked. Or was Brice ashamed? Embarrassed? Or simply that private a person?

Whatever the case, Karen wasn't about to betray his trust. Particularly when they were getting along. Particularly when she still needed his help.

So the dilemma was what to tell Meg. "Rowena is a lovely woman. I don't think she has a personal secretary...unless she's been hiding things from me all this time.'' Intent on redirecting the discussion, she asked, ''What else does Dr. Carlin have you do—'' she dropped her eyes to the tray ''—besides making great breakfasts?''

Meg looked around the room. ''I do laundry, dust, vacuum....'' Her gaze lit on the dresser, the small table by the chair, the nightstand, and she frowned. ''Where are your things?'' She looked quickly back to read Karen's answer.

''At home. I hadn't planned on being sick.''

''Where's home?''

''Syracuse.''

Meg nodded, then frowned when she glanced down at the tray. ''You're not eating.''

''I'm talking.''

''I'd leave you alone, but Dr. Carlin said I was to stay and make sure you finish. Maybe if I just sit here,'' she left the bedpost and went to the rocker, ''and look out the window, you can do it.''

Sure enough, she sat and looked out the window. Karen knew that if she were to speak, Meg's hearing aid would pick up the sound and the girl would turn around to read her lips. But Karen didn't speak. Dismaying as it was, she was actually feeling fatigued. Her voice was less hoarse than it had been, but it wasn't back to normal. Producing sound still took some effort, and she'd made enough of that for a while.

So she let the silence ride and concentrated on eating. It didn't take many forkfuls to fill her, but still she ate more. She didn't want to disappoint Meg, or suggest that the food wasn't good, or worse, risk Meg having to report to Brice that she'd failed at the job he'd given her.

In time, though, she reached her limit. "Meg?"

The girl's head came around, eyebrows raised in that same "pardon me" expression Karen had seen before. Then she stood and went to the bed to study the single sausage, half slice of toast and shreds of potato that remained on the plate. "That'll do until lunch."

"Lunch?" Karen echoed. The amount she'd just eaten for breakfast was more than she usually had for breakfast and lunch combined.

Meg didn't catch the dismay in her voice. "Dr. Carlin doesn't ask me to cook much, but I love doing it. While you're here, I'll have an excuse."

"Uh, please, Meg, don't plan. I don't know how long I can stay."

"Dr. Carlin said you'd be here for a while."

"Dr. Carlin may be wrong."

"I hope not. I really do like cooking. I was thinking of making quiche for lunch. I had some on my honeymoon—Richie took me to Atlantic City—but he says quiche isn't a man's food." She picked up the tray and continued to talk as she turned. "Man's food, woman's food—the cookbook says to use eggs and cheese and bacon, and those things would be nourishing for anybody—"

"Meg?" Karen said, but the young woman went on.

"—whether it's a man or a woman. But since Richie doesn't want it, you and I can—"

"*Meg*." This time, Meg turned. Knowing that the girl could see her lips, Karen lowered her voice. "How are the roads?"

"Wet. The sun is melting the snow."

"Is everything getting back to normal?"

"I think so."

"Do you think I would be able to get a cab?"

"I know you would. I passed two this morning."

Karen sank back against the pillows. There was one more critical question to ask. "Have you seen my clothes?"

Meg eyed her blankly. "Your clothes? No, I haven't seen them."

Karen's mind instantly replayed the theory that Brice was holding her prisoner by keeping her naked—or nearly so. She was going to have to confront him again. "I'm sure they're around," she mumbled, then said more clearly, "Thanks for the breakfast. It was delicious."

With a smile and the tiniest curtsy, Meg left the room.

Karen slept. She awoke at noon wanting a bath, but not wanting to exert the energy to take one. The matter was solved when Meg came in with lunch—indeed a quiche that was quite good. Karen didn't have the heart to mention the number of eggs she'd eaten that day. There was also fresh-baked bread and a salad, and Karen felt so full afterward that she rolled right over and went back to sleep.

She awoke at three o'clock perfectly disgusted with herself for having accomplished absolutely nothing. Pushing herself up against the pillows, she brooded, and the longer she did that, the more disgusted she felt. Not only had she accomplished nothing, but Brice hadn't been in once to see her.

She wondered why. He'd been so attentive over the weekend. She knew that he was working, but it wasn't as though his office was in town. It was in the other wing of the house. If he'd wanted to, he could have easily stopped up between appointments to check on her.

So much for country doctors making house calls, she mused a bit petulantly. For all *he* knew she was worse. In fact, she did feel warmer than she had at noon and suspected that her temperature was back up, though not by much. But Brice didn't know that. For all he knew she was burning up with fever. For all *he* knew, she'd gotten dressed and left the house!

Of course, he had her clothes—or knew where they were.

But she wasn't fussy. She didn't have to wear her own clothes to leave.

With the gears of her mind starting to turn, she climbed from bed, went out into the hall and looked both ways. There were doors to either side, lots of doors. She spent only a minute wondering why a man who lived alone would have a house with so many rooms. Then she started to explore.

The first door opened into a room that was totally empty. The second door likewise. The third door opened into Brice's room. It was larger than the others—including hers—by nearly double. A speedy look at the placement of doors and windows told her that he had indeed combined two rooms to form this one.

Done in navies and grays with a far simpler decor than the guest room, his bedroom was as masculine as the man himself. The bed, which was covered with a plaid quilt, was large and low. A lacquered headboard extended from the left nightstand to the right one. On that right one, was a telephone.

Making straight for it, she raised the receiver, brought it to her ear, lowered it to her chest for a minute, then set it down. There was no point calling a cab until she knew she had something to wear. So she returned her attention to the room.

The carpet was gray and plush. Navy Levelors covered the windows and were pulled high to let in the light of the day. There was a low dresser and an armoire, both of the same navy as the bed set. But the rest of the closets were built in—an entire wall's worth.

Karen headed for that wall. Drawing one door open, she found a sparse collection of suits and dress shoes. Closing that and moving to the next, she found shelves for shirts that were neatly pressed and folded. She figured that she could easily take one without it being missed, but she couldn't quite get herself to do it. They looked so neat, so proper, so starched. Closing that section of the closet, she opened the next. It held a television and a VCR, and the shelf above was filled with video cassettes. Unable to resist, she tipped her head and read some of the titles. There were classics and contemporaries, most of a serious or artsy bent. It was an impressive collection—as was the musical one on a lower shelf below the stereo.

But she felt too much like a thief to browse. Hastily shutting that door, she moved along to find shelves of sweaters. After a quick perusal, she took what appeared to be one of the older ones and hugged it to her chest while she examined the next section, which held the corduroy jeans Brice wore all the time.

She stared at the jeans. That was it. Jeans, a sweater, maybe a pair of socks. She was sure she'd find her boots and coat in the closet downstairs. It would be very simple. She'd dress and be gone.

Still she stood. And as she stood, she found that the thought of sneaking out of Brice's home wasn't half as appealing, now that she had the means, as it had been before. She wanted her own clothes, her own car.

And she wanted Brice's blessing.

Of course, she wouldn't get it, she decided. He would remind her that she was still sick, remind her of how she'd fainted in the snow, remind her of her buried car and her deferred jobs. He wouldn't remind her about the midterms that were on the horizon, because that would defeat his purpose. But he would be very sane, very sensible, very dogmatic about the rest.

Still she wanted to see him.

Disappointed that she didn't have the guts, but knowing that she couldn't function any other way, she silently returned the sweater to its shelf, checked to see that the closet doors were all closed, gave a last wistful glance at the phone and left the room.

She was standing in the middle of her own, wondering what kind of fool she was, when Meg knocked and entered. She carried a small tray this time, with more hot chocolate, an orange cut into slices and three very large oatmeal-raisin cookies. A shopping bag was dangling from her elbow.

Ignoring the fact that Karen stood stock still in the middle of the room, she set the tray down on the nightstand, then held out the bag.

"From Dr. Carlin."

Karen stared at the bag and frowned, at which point Meg went to her and pressed the twine handles into her palm.

"He went to Chelsea's," she said excitedly.

Karen could see where he'd been. The distinctive pale green and violet bag could have come from no other store. She couldn't count the number of times she'd admired the window of the Syracuse branch. She'd never gone in, though. The prices were exorbitant.

Meg rolled to her tiptoes and made a peeking movement toward the bag, silently urging Karen to open it. Karen did. Inside were several items, each wrapped in pale green tissue that matched the bag. She opened the first to find a hairbrush, but it was like none she'd ever owned. It was imported and of the finest boar bristles set in a sterling silver body with a handle to match.

Meg made soft ooo-ing sounds.

Karen was more cautious. She didn't know what to make of the gift. Brice had already done enough. She felt awkward.

Brush in one hand and bag in the other, she sat down on the edge of the bed. For another minute, she admired the brush's beauty. Then she gently set it down and looked into the bag again. This time she unwrapped a pair of deep red, fuzzy slippers.

Draped around the bedpost now, Meg clapped her hands.

Karen ran her fingers through the soft fur, brought it to her cheek for a minute, then set the slippers down beside the brush. The next package was small and light. She held her breath, deathly afraid that she'd find a lacy nightgown, and if that were the case, she couldn't possibly keep it. The suggestiveness would be too much.

Rather than a lacy nightgown, though, she eased aside the tissue to find a lightweight knit nightshirt with Mickey Mouse on the front.

"How fun!" Meg cried.

Karen was more confused than ever. A sterling silver hairbrush was very much Brice's style. Furry slippers and a Mickey Mouse nightshirt weren't. Doubly curious, she dug into the bag for the largest and last bundle. It contained a deep red terry velour robe to match the slippers.

"Try them on," Meg begged. "See how they look."

Karen was sitting on the bed, head bowed, eyes on the gifts. "Why did he do this?" she asked no one in particular.

Meg touched her shoulder with a single finger, then crouched down, silently asking that Karen repeat what she'd said so that she could read her lips.

"I think I'd like to take a bath first," Karen said.

Meg's gaze traveled to the tray on the nightstand, forgotten in the excitement.

"I think I'll take a bath second," Karen amended when she was sure Meg could see. "First I'll eat."

She was buying time. Before she put on the things Brice had bought, she had to be sure she was doing the right thing. So she nibbled at the cookies and sipped the cocoa and thought. She sucked out an orange slice, took another bite of cookie and thought. She sipped more, nibbled more, sucked more. But no amount of thinking could provide a definitive answer to her dilemma for the simple reason that she didn't know Brice's mind. She had no idea why he'd bought her anything, much less such lovely gifts. The hairbrush, the robe and slippers spoke for themselves. But she thought the Mickey Mouse nightshirt lovely, too. It was fun and carefree in a way she'd been only for one short time in her life. It made her want to be that way again.

Meg left on the pretense of ironing sheets. Needing a diversion from her thoughts, Karen went in search of the bath she'd been thinking about. She ended up taking a shower, because the glass-enclosed stall was too much to resist, as was the promise of endless hot water. Her own apartment had a showerless tub, and more often than not, the hot water was used up by the landlord, who lived below her with his wife and four kids and *did* have a shower, which was constantly in use. Brice's shower, on the other hand, was divine. It was large and bright, and the water pressure couldn't have been better. When she emerged she felt as though she'd been handled by a personal masseuse.

She was back in bed, toweling her hair, when Meg returned. Without a word, the girl picked up the brush, gently nudged Karen's hands aside and went to work.

If the shower had been heaven, that brushing was a step beyond. Karen had taken showers before. But it had been years, *years* since anyone had leisurely brushed her hair. Eyes closed, she savored one long stroke after the next until she was sure she'd liquify.

She didn't liquify, though. She fell asleep as soon as Meg left. This time when she awoke, Brice was there.

She was lying halfway on her side, with her cheek on the pillow and her upper arm stretched out on the quilt. As soon as she stirred, she sensed his presence, a large immovable object by her hip.

Slowly she opened her eyes. He was sitting on the side of the bed, with his elbows on his knees, hands hanging loosely between. Only his head was turned her way, and though the pose should have been awkward, he looked as though he'd been there a while and could well sit a while longer.

She didn't know what to do. The last time she'd seen him had been the evening before, and the heat that had passed between them was as fresh in her mind as if she'd dreamed it that minute. In fact, she wondered if she had. The air around her felt charged with the same sensual awareness. It didn't help that he was so close, or that he was looking dark and mysterious in a black sweater and charcoal cords. Dark and mysterious was handsome—with the slight shadow of a beard on his cheek, very handsome. And he was just sitting there, watching her, thinking his own dark and mysterious and private thoughts.

She had no way of knowing that the reason he didn't move was because he didn't know what to do, either.

He had been stunned when he'd entered the room to find her sleeping. She was wearing the nightshirt he'd bought, and the robe was at the foot of the bed, the slippers on the floor—all of which gave him a feeling of satisfaction. But what stunned him was her looks. In all his years as a doctor, he'd never seen quite the change that three days of rest could make as he saw in Karen. Her skin was soft and smooth, still pale but more naturally so. The bags under her eyes had shrunk to shadows. Her features had relaxed. But her hair was what stopped him dead. It was breathtaking.

For one thing, it fell in long, thick curls over her shoulders to her back. For another it shone. For a third, whatever she'd used to wash it had brought out golden highlights on a field of pecan. The whole thing looked lighter. It looked alive.

In point of fact it scared him a little, but he'd be damned if he'd let that show. He had to have the upper hand when it came to Karen. So he schooled his expression to one of complete control.

Karen, meanwhile, was feeling awkward. "Thank you for the things," she said in a quiet voice. "You didn't have to do that."

"You needed a brush."

"A five-and-dime model would have been fine."

"Don't you like the silver one?"

"Yes, but it's too much."

"I can't return it now. You've already used it."

"I know." She felt his gaze on her hair, smoothing, stroking, separating the long curls, exploring them. Her scalp hummed. It boggled her mind to think what would happen if he actually touched her hair with his hand. He'd done it the night before, but in offer of comfort when she'd been upset. She had something else in mind now.

And that wasn't right at all. She had to leave.

Annoyed at herself, her tone was suitably cross. "You've avoided me so I wouldn't be able to nag you about leaving."

That was only one of the reasons Brice had avoided her. The other was that he'd felt too much when he'd faced her the night before. It was one thing to be touched by her helplessness, to feel sorry that she was ill, to do whatever he could to ease her physical distress. It was another to desire her. He'd wanted to make some sense of that in his mind before he faced her again. So he'd sent Meg with her food, her pills, the things he'd bought her in town. And he'd checked by for regular reports—but from Meg, not Karen.

At some point in the course of the afternoon, though, he'd realized that if he didn't face Karen, she was apt to walk out. He was surprised she hadn't tried it already. The fact that he'd taken her clothes would stall her, but not stop her. If she was like Rowena, she'd find a way to do whatever she set her mind to. He intended to stay one step ahead of that.

Without acknowledging her accusation one way or the other, he asked, "How are you feeling?"

"Better."

"Meg said you were warm again this afternoon."

"Meg has sharp eyes."

"Were you?"

"A little. I'm fine now."

He could see it. Her skin was the color of cream and very soft. He also saw the way her lips were slightly parted, the way her eyes were alert. She hadn't moved since she'd awoken and seemed as wary of him as he was of himself. That meant she remembered what had passed between them, too. He wondered what she'd do if he did reach out to touch her.

Brice fell back to the one sure thing in his life. "A slight rise in temperature isn't unusual with something like this, especially late in the afternoon. It may go up and down for several days."

"Then it's something I can monitor myself." Rolling to her back, she eyed him in earnest. "I have to get home, Brice. Meg says the roads are melting, so someone should be able to get at my car. The receptionist at the nursing home—Judy—said that her brother is great with cars and that if I ever have a problem, she'll be glad to have him take a look."

Brice was focusing on her face, but still he noticed the swell of her breasts beneath the nightshirt. "It was the battery. It couldn't be salvaged, so I had them put in a new one, and if you can't afford it, I can."

"I can afford it."

"I thought you were poor."

"Not that poor. I have an emergency fund."

"If you have an emergency fund, why your panic at the thought of not working for a while?"

"Because an emergency fund should be used only in an emergency. Not working to lie around in bed isn't an emergency."

"Not working to recover from pneumonia and exhaustion is an emergency."

"So I realized," she said quietly and was rewarded for her humility when Brice was momentarily without a comeback. She took the advantage to press her point. "That doesn't mean I can stay here. I have too much work to do. If I were home, I could be reading, writing my paper, studying."

He was quick to rally. "That's exactly what you'd be doing if you were home. You'd be pushing yourself harder than ever to catch up, then get ahead, and you still need sleep. I've been sitting here for half an hour. You were dead to the world.''

"Half an hour?'' The thought of his watching her made her uneasy. "That must have been boring.''

"No.''

She waited for him to go on. He didn't. His gaze dropped, leaving a trail of tingles from her chin, down her neck and chest to the small black bulb of Mickey Mouse's nose. Beneath that bulb was her nipple. It tightened instantly.

Dismayed, Karen debated her options. She could either draw the quilt to her throat, or sit up. If Brice was in a lecherous mood, he'd know exactly what she was doing and why. Then again, she'd never seen him in a lecherous mood. Dangerous, yes. Angry and frustrated, yes. Even sexually aware…

She sat up *and* tugged the quilt higher, deciding that she'd rather be safe than sorry. She also decided that it was time she stated her intent. "I'd like to stay the night, but if you'll give me my things, I can write you a check and be on my way in the morning.''

He straightened, flexed his shoulders, closed his eyes, rocked his head around on his neck. Karen thought he looked like a fighter preparing for the next round. She was surprised when, rather than attacking her, he gave the floor a contemplative look. "Rowena called wanting to know how you were. She told me I wasn't to let you leave until you were completely well.''

"Do you always do what she tells you to do?''

He looked at her in a way that left no doubt as to his answer. He was not the obedient type.

But Karen had sensed that from the start. "Then she won't be shocked when you discharge me early," she said.

"I'm not discharging you. If you leave, it will be against my wishes."

She thought about that for a minute, then offered a quiet, if unrepentant, "I'm sorry."

"What if I don't give you your clothes?"

"I'll take yours. You have a whole stack of sweaters. You could spare one for a day or two."

He turned to face her, his eyes dark, unreadable. "You were in my bedroom."

She swallowed. He was so close. So large. "That's right."

"What did you think?"

"What did I think?" she echoed dumbly.

"Of the bedroom."

"You mean, what did I think of the way it looked?"

"What else would I mean?" he asked impatiently.

She'd been prepared to defend herself against charges of trespassing. Taken off guard, she shrugged and sat back against the headboard. "I thought it was very neat and clean."

"The decoration."

"Oh. That. It was nice. Your wall of closets is fantastic. That whole room used to be two, didn't it?"

He gave a quick nod. "This used to be a tavern."

"Really?" she asked, instantly charmed. It made

sense, now that she thought about it—the setup of rooms downstairs, their abundance on the second floor and in the wing.

Brice was entranced by the tiny curl at the corner of her mouth. It was rare, tempting. So while his eyes didn't budge from that spot, he went on a little about the house.

"It's certified. I have papers. This place used to be a famous watering hole."

"For humans."

"And horses."

"Not inside."

"Obviously. The public part of the tavern was in the three large rooms downstairs. The rooms up here were…I'm not sure…rented out, I guess."

There was an undercurrent to his vagueness that gave Karen pause. There was also the flicker of something in his eyes—she thought maybe it was discomfort, though it was fast gone. She tried to picture the house as a tavern, tried to imagine the downstairs rooms filled with carousers and the upstairs rooms, one after another along the hall, filled with…filled with…people…doing…what?

Her face lit up as she proudly announced, "It was a brothel, wasn't it?"

"I didn't say that."

"But it was."

He could swear he saw a smile. It was small, crooked, even rusty. But it did look like a smile. And it set off a burst of heat in his veins. "Does that please you?"

Her eye twinkled. "It's an...amusing idea. You're so dark and serious and straight. The good doctor. A pillar of the community. The thought of your living in a whorehouse—"

"Former whorehouse."

"Former whorehouse." Her smile didn't widen, and it was still crooked, but her lips were more relaxed, as though they were getting used to it. "That's rich."

If she was laughing at him, Brice didn't mind. Two could play the game as well as one. "If it's true, do you know what it means?"

"Sure." She looked around the room. "It means that the decor in here must have been a sight different then than it is now."

"Uh-huh. Flashier. Sleazier. Lots of furniture, maybe a folding screen in the corner with flimsy little outfits hanging over the top."

Or mirrors on the ceiling, Karen thought, shooting a glance in that direction.

Brice followed her thought with ease. "It means that this room has seen its share of action." He flattened a hand on the bed on the far side of her hips, penning her in. "Think about it, Karen. All that loving in this bed."

Karen's smile was fading fast. He was too close. Too real. Too large. Too manly. "Not loving. Sex."

"Okay. Sex."

"And not in this bed."

He conceded that with a negligent, one-shouldered shrug. There was nothing negligent about his expression. "Okay, another bed. But in this spot. Wild, hot sex. Over and over, night after night."

"You have an incredible imagination," she murmured, but her breath caught, because his eyes weren't to be believed. They were dark, hypnotic, seductive. He was looking at her as though she could have been the object of that wild, hot sex. "Don't look at me that way," she whispered.

"What way?" His voice was a little hoarse. It rubbed against her, heightening the sexual tension she felt.

"That way."

"I'm just looking at you."

"You're hungry."

"My, we're direct."

Flattening herself against the headboard, she hugged her arms to her chest and murmured a bit frantically, "I need room, Brice. You're crowding me."

But Brice moved closer. He was feeling an irresistible urge to kiss her, and this time he wasn't going to deny himself. She was determined to leave; he wanted to taste her before she did. And besides, he could swear, could swear that despite her protests, she was hungry, too.

"Brice…"

He took her wrists and, uncrossing her arms, drew her forward.

"Brice…please, Brice. I'm not well," she reasoned, but her voice was without force. "Haven't you been saying so for days on end?"

He drew her closer. "Not days on end. Three days. And for far too much of that time I've been wondering about this." Bracing her back with his forearm, he took her face in his hand. Then, just when Karen was opening her mouth to protest, he covered it with his own.

6

Karen fought him. Calling on what little strength she had, she tried to push him away, but he was rock solid. She twisted her body, tried to turn her head, but he held it firm. She whimpered into his mouth, but he didn't yield.

Then she went still. Since fighting hadn't worked, she decided she had nothing to lose by stopping, lying motionless in his arms, holding her mouth rigid beneath his. No man wanted to kiss a stone.

That was the plan, and in theory it was sound. But it was self-defeating, because without fighting, her senses were open to what Brice was doing.

He was very slowly, very purposefully caressing her mouth. His touch was firm and willful, but gentle in an oddly masculine kind of way. He slanted his lips across hers, opening them to draw her soft flesh to his warmth. He sipped. He sucked. He tasted her as he would a fine wine, swirling her lips in his mouth, savoring their bouquet.

Karen had never been savored quite that way before. Her breath came faster. Without conscious thought, she relaxed her lips. Her skin warmed. The fine network of nerve ends that radiated outward from her mouth was reinforced at each spot where her body touched his. But the starburst went deeper. She felt a heat she'd never known in her very core. The urge to melt was terrifying.

That was what Brice saw in her eyes when he reluctantly freed her mouth. His face was inches above hers, his gaze fixed on those eyes before falling to her lips, which were soft, faintly swollen and moist. He wanted to taste more; the need was alive in every pore of his body. But that look of fear in her eyes kept him from it.

He didn't want her afraid when he kissed her. He wanted her warm and eager. For that matter, he wanted her warm and eager for life in general, yet she wasn't. She was running on a treadmill, too busy keeping the pace to consider what it was worth.

She never smiled. He wanted to see her smile— and not smugly at the thought of his house having once been a brothel. He wanted to see her smile in pure delight. In innocent pleasure, sheer fun, unadulterated joy.

Splaying his fingers on either side of her head, he spoke in a deep, rumbling voice that held quiet command. "You're staying here, Karen. I promised Rowena I'd care for you, and I mean to do it. Early tomorrow morning, I'll drive you back to Syracuse. You can pick up your books, pens, papers, clothes, anything else you need to have to function here for a while."

"But—"

He covered her lips with his thumbs. "I have a typewriter and a computer if you want either. You know as well as I do that you can get class notes from someone else, but if you insist on going to classes yourself, I'll have you driven there and back. It should be no worse than the trips you've made to the nursing home, and with someone else driving, you can rest. You can study for midterms; you can go back and take them. Then you have a vacation. I want you here till it's over.''

''I can't—''

He renewed the pressure of his thumbs. ''You can. And you will.'' His dark eyes held hers for a minute longer, reinforcing the order. Then he released her and rose from the bed. He didn't look back on his way to the door. He didn't say another word.

Nor did Karen as she silently watched his tall frame pass from sight. Only when the rapid tattoo of his footsteps on the stairs faded did she release her breath. She put her fingertips to her lips. She dropped her gaze to the floor. A bewildered look appeared on her face.

She should have spoken up. She should have argued. But she hadn't, and she knew why.

She wanted to stay.

Lifting her gaze, she sent it slowly around the room, touching on each piece of furniture, each small decorative item. Her mind's eye wandered down the stairs to the living room, with its corduroy sofa and its blazing hearth, then to the other rooms, with their warm, dark wood, then to the kitchen with ultramodern amenities that were somehow traditionalized.

It would be so easy to stay, she mused. Whorehouse or not, she loved what she'd seen of the house. Even the powder room, which she'd seen only when she'd been so sick, left an impression of burgundy and cream in paisley walls, ceramic fixtures and stained glass sconces. It was warm here. Quiet. She'd never spent any time in a home that was quite as comfortable.

Then there was the fact that Brice made her feel safe. But he also threatened her. She couldn't stay if he planned to remind her of the accident at every turn. She couldn't stay if he planned to lecture her about her life-style. And she *certainly* couldn't stay if he planned to kiss her often—or could she? He had given her a taste of delicious feelings. She wondered where they'd lead.

Swinging her legs over the side of the bed, she slid her feet into her slippers, freshened up in the bathroom, secured her hair with its customary barettes, then wrapped herself in the deep red robe and went looking for Brice.

It was easy this time. Not only was the noise in the kitchen a dead giveaway, but she could smell something cooking. It was strong—either that or she was greatly improved, because whatever it was successfully penetrated her nasal passages. It was also Italian and tempting enough to make her salivate.

Brice spared her little more than a glance when she appeared at the kitchen door. He had a mitt on his hand and was busily shifting things around in the wall oven. Karen, whose father had never gone near a stove, was intrigued. She wasn't sure how Brice could manage to cook and look masculine at the same time, but he did.

Then she remembered how he'd kissed her. She hadn't watched him while he was doing it, so she didn't know how he'd looked, but she'd felt him. She'd felt his firm mouth on hers, felt his large hands holding her face, felt his muscled chest exerting pressure on her breasts. He'd felt plenty masculine then.

She was unaware of the flare of pink on her cheeks, but Brice wasn't. Nor was he unaware of how captivating she looked in the robe he'd bought—or how quickly his body could respond to both the flare and the captivation. He never should have kissed her, *never* should have kissed her, but he'd been provoked. He'd been a little curious, a little belligerent, a little aroused. Unfortunately, now he was a little confused. And a lot horny.

So he concentrated on getting supper. With the garlic bread stowed beside the lasagna, he closed the oven door and went to take plates from an overhead cabinet. He shot a glance at Karen. She was standing with her arms around her waist and her eyes on the floor. He followed her gaze, thinking that maybe he'd spilled something, but the adobe tile was as clean as it had been after Meg had mopped it that afternoon.

"You should be in bed," he said gruffly. Putting the plates on the counter, he opened another cabinet.

She looked up. "We have to talk."

"That's not a good idea." He set down two glasses and closed the cabinet. "We don't see eye to eye on many things."

"Brice, you can't just give orders and have them obeyed."

He rummaged around in the silverware drawer. "Why not?"

"Because thinking people don't take to dictatorships."

Two forks slid over the counter to the plates. "It didn't strike me that you were doing much thinking when you worked yourself into pneumonia, then went to visit Rowena and passed out in the snow. Besides, this isn't a dictatorship. It's a democracy that is temporarily under martial law. I'm the doctor. I know what's best."

"Oh, please," Karen muttered.

He met her gaze. "I do."

"You know what's best for *you*, but that may not be what's best for me. And don't tell me that the AMA would approve of your prescription in this case, because I doubt it would."

Brice crossed to the refrigerator, which took him close enough to Karen for her to have to look up. He opened the door, then paused and eyed her. "Are you planning to report me to the AMA?"

"Of course not."

"That's good, because you wouldn't have much of a case." Turning his attention back to the refrigerator, he removed a large salad bowl and set it on the counter. "What's happening between us is personal."

Karen didn't waste her breath with denials. "That's why we have to talk. You're asking me to live here with you for the next month, but how can I do that, when I barely know you?''

''Dressing?''

She blinked. ''Excuse me?''

''Do you take your salad with dressing?''

''Of course.''

''What kind?''

''I'm not fussy.''

''What kind?''

''Whatever you're having.''

''What kind?''

''Thousand Island.''

''Thank you,'' he said. He took a bottle of Thousand Island dressing from the shelf on the inside of the refrigerator door, then closed the door and turned to the counter. There he busied himself filling two salad plates from the larger bowl. He was using his hands; they worked far better than salad tongs.

Karen had no objection to that, but as she stood watching him work, she realized that her legs were tiring. She glanced at the kitchen table. It was oak and inlaid with tiles. Four chairs, two on a side, were of the same oak with sturdy rush seats. She made her way to one and sat down.

''Are you sure you're up to this?'' Brice asked without turning.

''Yes. That's why your insisting that I stay here for a month is so bizarre. I'm fine. Really.''

''Don't give me that.''

''It's true. Okay, I'm not one hundred percent, but

I'm on the mend. I'm no worse now than if I had a bad cold."

Mitts in hand, Brice took the lasagna from the oven and set it on the counter. "You're weaker, and that won't go away in a day. You'll be tired over the next few weeks. Your temperature may go up and down. Your cough should be watched." He tossed the mitts into a drawer. "Do you know what would happen if you stopped taking penicillin?"

"I'd get sick again."

He nodded.

"But I don't have to stop taking it," Karen pointed out. "You could give me a prescription. I'm not even contagious anymore."

Taking a bottle of milk from the refrigerator, he filled the glasses and put them on the table. They were followed shortly by the salad, replete with healthy toppings of dressing. Closemouthed and stony-eyed, he started doling out the lasagna.

At that point, Karen sensed that he had no intention of arguing further. He'd decided what should be done; he felt added discussion unnecessary. In a way, that was fine with her. She hadn't come downstairs to argue. She'd come to learn about the man who had appointed himself her guardian.

Starting with something relatively neutral, she asked, "How long have you lived here?"

Brice tried to find a catch to the question. At length he decided it was innocent enough. "Nine years."

"Was it a home when you bought it?"

He set a serving of lasagna before her. "You mean, as opposed to a whorehouse?"

So much for neutrality. "I was only guessing about that. Was someone living here when you bought it?"

"Yes."

She waited. Instead of elaborating, he retrieved the garlic bread from the oven. So she bluntly asked, "Who?"

He made a production of peeling back the foil, cutting the bread into slices, piling them in a basket. "The Walkers."

"The Walkers. Ahh. That says it all."

He shot her a wry glance. "The Walkers were a professional couple, both teaching at Cornell. They had seven kids and two maids. The house was perfect for them." Tossing the basket on the table, he went back to the counter for his own plate.

"Seven kids. Incredible. Why did they sell?"

"They received appointments at Stanford."

"Why did you buy?"

He sat down directly across from her. "Because I liked the place. I liked the location, I liked the land, I liked the house."

"But it's so big. You don't have seven kids and two maids. You don't have a wife, for that matter."

"I have an office. And a large practice." He raised his milk. "That requires a certain amount of space." He took a healthy drink.

Karen didn't miss the gentle bob of his Adam's apple when the milk went down. His neck was solid, not thick, but nicely developed. She wondered if he worked out.

"Were you practicing here in Ithaca before you bought the house?" she asked.

He picked up his fork. "I had an office in town and was living in an apartment not far from there."

"But you had a dream," she said anticipatorily.

"Don't we all?"

She wondered about his somberness, but sensed there'd be a better time to explore it. "We don't all get to fulfill our dreams. You did. You dreamed of working out of your home. Now you are."

Brice set down the fork and stared at her straight. "I worked hard to get where I am. The one break I had was that I didn't graduate from med school in debt. Rowena saw to that. But she couldn't wave a magic wand and make a successful practice appear. I had to work my butt off for that."

"I'm sure you did," Karen replied in a conciliatory voice, but he wasn't done.

"I started out in hospitals and clinics. Three or four times a week I spent my nights in emergency rooms. I covered for every other doctor in the area until, little by little, my name spread. I've paid my dues. I've earned more regular hours and the right to leave my own patients with a covering physician and go away several times a year."

Apparently, she'd struck a raw chord. She hadn't meant to do that, but it was interesting—a little clue as to what made the man tick. It seemed he was sensitive about what he had and what he'd had to do to get it. He was proud of his achievements—as rightly he should be, she reflected. But he was also defensive. She wondered why.

But she wasn't up to asking. That was sure to bring on a fight, and she didn't want one. So she settled for a sincere, "I think it's wonderful that you were able to buy this house."

Brice stared at his plate for a long minute before lifting his fork and starting to eat. After several more minutes, he took a breath and said more quietly, "Anyway, when this place came on the market, I knew the setup was right. Separate wing, separate entrance for my patients. Plenty of room for me."

"And Rowena?"

He leveled her a stare. "What about Rowena?"

She weathered the stare as best she could, while she asked herself why innocent comments should set him off. "Did she ever live here with you?"

"No."

"Or visit?"

"Sometimes."

The obvious question, of course, was why Rowena wasn't with him now. Brice had the money to hire a nurse, and he had room to house them both. If he cared as much for his grandmother as he implied he did, why was she in a nursing home?

Karen knew better than to ask. "Do you entertain much?"

"No."

"Have out-of-town friends in to visit?"

"No."

"Oh." She couldn't quite figure out what he wanted with all the upstairs rooms. The obvious answer was that he was planning on having a family of his own one day. But if that were true, what was he waiting for? He had a huge house and a successful practice. And he wasn't getting any younger.

"Have you ever been married?" she asked.

He set down his fork again and looked pointedly at hers, which she hadn't touched. "Aren't you going to eat?"

"I will."

"Not if you're talking. Doesn't your mouth ever stop?"

"I'm only asking questions."

"Well, can it."

"Why?"

"Because it's annoying. Shut your mouth for a change."

Karen didn't feel she deserved his sharpness, but if he could shell it out, so could she. "How do you propose I get food in if I do that?"

"You'll find a way."

Sitting back in her chair, she looked at him in dismay. "I hope you know that your personality leaves something to be desired."

"So I've been told."

"It's not critical that I eat right now. You just didn't want to answer my question."

"If you don't eat now, the lasagna will get cold. Meg made it for you."

"And for you."

But he shook his head. "She knows that I don't care one way or another what I eat."

"Poor Meg. She should be working someplace where she can be appreciated. I hope you don't tell her that the sauce is too thin."

"I don't, because it's not, and if it were, I wouldn't say a thing. Meg is special."

That was what Karen had figured. She rather envied Meg her "special" status. The sharpness of Brice's tongue smarted. Karen could still feel its sting. If Meg was spared that, she was blessed.

"It was kind of you to hire her," Karen said, thinking the comment innocent and sincere. She was startled when Brice bristled.

"Kind? It was practical. I needed someone; she was there. Believe me, she earns her wages."

"All right," Karen murmured hastily. "All right." Feeling more weary than she had moments before, she looked down at her food and began to eat. In the periphery of her vision, she saw Brice doing the same. She'd taken two mouthfuls of lasagna to his four when he set down his fork.

"I'm not angry at you," he said, frowning.

"Could've fooled me," she replied without looking up.

"I'm not. I just…get that way sometimes."

"Mmm. Angry."

"Not at you."

She did look up in challenge then. "You've been angry at me. Don't deny it. And what was so awful about my asking whether you've ever been married?

Is it a state secret? Rowena would tell me if I asked. And, by the way,'' she went on brashly, ''tomorrow's my day to visit her. I'm going.''

For several minutes, Brice said nothing. He stared at her, then calmly returned to his dinner. Only after he'd made his way through better than half of his meal did he look up again, shocking her this time with the shadow of a smile. ''You have spunk.''

''I have to have *something* to deal with you.''

''Most people turn and run.''

''Believe me, I would if I could, but I'm not exactly in shape. You'd catch me in a minute. And I can't run out in this weather wearing nothing but a robe. You have my clothes.''

''The dry cleaner has them.''

''Same difference.'' She snatched up a piece of bread, tore off a corner and ate it, but there the small burst of frustration-induced energy seemed to wane. Sitting back, she chewed more slowly.

''You're feeling tired, aren't you?'' Brice asked.

''I'm okay.''

His tone sharpened. ''Are you feeling tired?''

She met his gaze, but sadly, not defiantly. ''Yes.''

''Do you want to go back to bed?'' he asked on a gentler note.

''Soon.'' She took a small drink of milk, then nudged a piece of lettuce around the edge of her salad. When it hit a cherry tomato, she abandoned it and forked a small piece of lasagna toward the side of the dish. And all the while she was trying to decide whether Brice disliked her because she had hit Rowena or…just…because.

"How's the food?"

Her head came up with a start. "Just fine."

"Don't you like lasagna?"

"I love lasagna."

"Is it too spicy?"

"No, it's great."

"Then why are you picking at it like it's liver?"

With carefully controlled movements, she set down her fork. With as carefully controlled movements, she raised her head. And when she spoke, her voice was as carefully controlled as her movements had been.

"I'm picking," she said quietly, "because you've upset my stomach. I'm not used to eating, let alone in a war zone. I can understand why you live alone. If you do to other people what you do to me, not even a fool would want to be with you."

Her throat felt tight. She looked down at her lap, then back up. There was more to say. "What I don't understand is how you can be a doctor—" She held up a hand. "No, I take that back. I can understand it. You warm up to the sick just fine. How the *families* of the sick can stand you is beyond me, but maybe they're desperate enough for medical help that they can excuse the rudeness."

She took a quick breath. "I can't, Brice. I can't live with it, even if it's only for a month. For twenty-one years, I lived in a house filled with constant tension. I don't want that. I'd rather be alone." To her chagrin, her eyes began to tear. Swearing softly, she bowed her head and covered her face with a hand.

Brice sat very still. He watched her struggle for control and though he felt an intense urge to help her, he couldn't move. He hadn't meant to cause her pain—or maybe he had, but if so, he was sorry. He no longer saw her solely as the woman who had put Rowena in a wheelchair; she had feelings and a personality, both of which he found himself drawn to.

But if he'd wanted to get her to stay, he'd gone about it the wrong way. "Karen?"

Her head remained bowed. "I'm okay."

He opened his mouth, then closed it and swallowed. Then he tried again, this time producing quiet sound. "I'm a jackass."

"You can say that again."

"No. It was hard enough the first time. I'm not used to apologizing."

"That must be why you have so many friends."

"I'm not good with people."

"Sure," was her facetious reply. "You're a doctor and you're not good with people."

"I'm not."

She fiddled with the belt of her robe. "I could buy that if you were in research. But you have a successful practice. You said so yourself. So how do you do it? Are your patients masochists?"

"My patients are kids. I'm good with kids. Not adults."

Karen looked up in disbelief. "Kids?"

He nodded.

"You're a pediatrician?"

He had his forearms on the table. His fingers were curled, not fisted but tense. He wore a look of vulnerability, which only added to her disbelief.

"I am a pediatrician," he stated. "Is that so hard to believe?"

"Yes! I mean, children are the most helpless creatures in the world. You can't be gruff with them. You can't issue orders and walk out. You can't come across like a block of ice."

"I don't."

She raised her shoulders while her eyes darted blindly around the kitchen. "I assumed you were a general practitioner, an internist, maybe a dermatologist—"

He sputtered his opinion of that.

"But a pediatrician. That's incredible."

"I'm a good doctor."

She didn't doubt it for a minute. "But a *pediatrician*!"

He was sitting straighter, beginning to look offended. "You don't have to act as though I'm the least likely candidate for the job, because I assure you I'm not. There are less likely candidates on the staff of every major children's hospital in the country. And I'm not that unlikely a candidate. I know what I'm doing medically, and I like kids.

"And what's more," he went on vehemently, "they like me. They don't have preconceived notions of what a doctor should be. They don't give a damn whether I belong to the university club or go to the local charity ball or pick up the award for 'Mr. Congeniality' at the state fair each year. They don't fault me because I choose to live alone. They don't ask for one iota more than I can give, which is the best medical care possible.''

Karen continued to study him, now with a bemused look on her face. "A pediatrician," she murmured. It took some getting used to, but the more she turned it over and around in her mind, the more she liked it. A slow, tentative smile touched her lips. "I think that's just fine," she said.

The smile, oh, the smile. It made Brice forget about being offended, made him forget about defending his specialty. That smile was a soothing balm flowing through his veins. It warmed his insides, made him want to bloom.

"Do you treat kids of all ages?" Karen asked softly.

He nodded.

"Even newborns?" she asked with a bit of awe. When he nodded again, she tried to picture his holding a tiny bundle of life. At first, she couldn't. Then she tried harder and slowly formed the image of his large hands cradling an infant. It was an unexpectedly beautiful idea and held her momentarily speechless.

"I've always had a laid-back approach to medicine," Brice said. "I know when to be alarmed, but I'm not an alarmist. I assume that's why mothers bring their kids to me."

Karen nodded.

"I mean," he went on with a sudden breath, "I

can relate to kids. I can sympathize with what they're feeling. They're guileless. Spontaneous. They say what's on their minds. They're honest without being malicious. I guess that's it. They can tell you they hate you. And at a particular moment—like when you've just given them a shot—they do, but they're not trying to hurt you back. They're not sophisticated enough for that.'' His mouth thinned. ''They don't learn that till they're older.''

He was suddenly dark again. Karen looked away, trying to retain in her mind's eye the warmer expression he'd been wearing when he'd been talking about his kids. And they were his kids. He saw them as his family. He hadn't said as much, but she'd heard it. His days were filled with the care of his kids, then he returned to his empty rooms at night.

It didn't make sense.

Lifting her fork, she picked at the lasagna for several minutes, but ate little. She was tired, no longer hungry, the lasagna was cold and Brice had her thoroughly confused.

''Brice?'' Her eyes went to his. ''Why do you dislike adults?''

He shrugged.

She pushed. ''Why?''

''Because they dislike me.''

''But why? I don't understand it.''

''That's not what you said a minute ago.''

''A minute ago I was angry. Now I don't know what to be.''

He sighed. "Look, Karen, it's no big thing. I like kids, so I work with kids."

"What about their parents?"

"What about them?"

"Children don't just walk into your office on their own. They're accompanied by adults, and those adults are the ones you converse with. How do you deal with them?"

"I deal with them. They bring their kids for medical care; I provide it. It's as simple as that."

Karen knew it wasn't, and her look told him so. "There's more to pediatrics than diagnosis and treatment. There are emotional issues in the rearing of a child. Doesn't a pediatrician have to address those, too?"

"I do."

"By telling a mother all she's doing wrong?"

"More often by telling her all she's doing right."

That shut Karen up for a minute. She hadn't expected that he'd give such a perfect answer. "What happens when a mother brings a child in with real behavioral problems?"

"I can tell pretty quickly whether I can help, and if I can't, I refer them to a specialist."

She couldn't find fault with that answer, either. "What about the mother who runs to your office every time her child sneezes? Or the one who refuses to follow the instructions you give her for the care of her child?"

"I can handle them, Karen. I may not like them, but I'm not a total social misfit. I know what's ex-

pected, and I give my version of it. I don't patronize.
I don't sweet-talk. And if they don't like that, they
go elsewhere.''

Apparently, Karen realized, they did like it, if
Brice's practice was as successful as he said. He cir-
cumvented his dislike of adults by dealing principally
with children; his love for and understanding of those
children soothed over any rough spots he might have
with their parents. What could be better?

She looked off toward the window. It was dark out.
Feeling a chill, she crossed her arms over her waist
and tucked her hands inside.

''Karen?''

Her gaze swung back.

''Are you all right?''

She nodded, but strange emotions whispered
through her as she looked at him. It occurred to her
that the stony expression he so often wore was part
of a barrier, part of a wall he erected to keep others
away and protect himself. Somewhere along the line
he'd been hurt. She felt badly.

''Your color's gone again,'' he observed.

''I'm okay.''

''I think you should go back to bed.''

''In a minute.'' In an odd way, she was enjoying
sitting with him. Yes, she felt tired. But she didn't
want to go back to bed just yet. ''I'm the first woman
who's ever stayed here, aren't I?'' she asked softly.

Brice didn't blink. ''Yes.''

''Why?''

''Why you? Or why no others?''

She shrugged, moved her head from side to side indicating that he could answer either or both.

Brice was feeling mellow. His kitchen was plenty big for two people, and he was finding that he liked Karen's company. He'd given her a hard time and still she stayed. Even after he'd told her to go to bed, she hadn't...and not out of defiance, either. Perhaps her illness had worn her down, but she'd softened. He almost got the impression that she liked his company, too, which was truly a miracle. He felt he owed her something for her perseverence.

"I was married once," he said in a voice that was only the slightest bit defensive. "It was right after I finished my residency. I figured that since I was going into private practice, it was time."

"Who was she?"

"An executive secretary at the hospital. I guess she figured it was time, too, and I was better than nothing."

"What an awful thing to say. Maybe she loved you."

"She thought she did."

"Did you love her?"

He considered that as he leaned back in his chair with one hand in his lap, the other on the table. He was giving the edge of his plate little flicks that rotated it by degrees. His features weren't as relaxed as the pose. "I thought I did, but I loved my work more. That frustrated her, so she made greater demands on my time and affection. We argued a lot. I took refuge in my work, and happily so. The divorce was amicable. She'd met someone else and wanted the quickest, cleanest split.''

"Oh."

His eyes met hers. ''What does that mean—'oh'?''

Karen shrugged. ''I don't know. I'd say I'm sorry, but you don't seem to be.''

"I'm not."

"But what about a family?"

"What about it?"

"You're a pediatrician. You love children. Don't you want to have some of your own?"

"Do you?" he asked.

She sank deeper in her chair simply because her body didn't want to hold her up. ''Some day.''

"You're not getting any younger."

"I was thinking the same about you. You're in a better position to have children than I am. You've made it. I still have a long way to go.'' She hooked a tired hand over her shoulder.

Brice couldn't help but note the limpness of that hand. ''I think you should go up.''

She closed her eyes for the space of several breaths. ''I'm not sure I can move from this chair.''

"Should I carry you?"

Her eyes opened, and she shook her head. ''I'd better be able to handle your stairs if I'm going to be able to manage three flights of mine tomorrow morning.''

Pushing his chair back, Brice stood, stacked the dishes, set the glasses on top and carried them all to the sink. ''So. What's the decision?'' he asked with his back to her as he directed a spray of water toward the plates. His voice was rougher. "Will you be staying here, or what?"

Karen studied his broad back, saw straight lines that verged on the rigid. "I didn't think you were giving me a choice."

He paused. "You have a choice."

"Do you want me to stay?"

"That's a dumb question," he barked. "Why else would I ask?"

"I don't know. But then, I don't know why you picked me up from the snow in the first place. Or why you've taken care of me for three days. Or why you bought me a nightshirt with Mickey Mouse on the front—why did you?"

Slowly he turned. "Would you have preferred something sexy?"

She shook her head.

"That's what I figured."

"So why Mickey Mouse?"

His gaze slid to her chest, settling on the spot where, beneath the deep red robe, the mouse's face would be. "Because it was sweet. And silly." His eyes rose and he rubbed the inside of his wrist against his pants. "Dumb, huh?"

She was more touched than she'd have believed possible. "No. I love it."

"But it hasn't made you smile."

"Maybe because it's more sweet than silly," she said, then gave him the smile he wanted. It was shy, not too big, but it was a smile nonetheless. "Thank you," she whispered. "I do love the nightshirt."

Not trusting his voice, Brice gave a single slow nod. At that moment, as he looked at Karen, he could find nothing, nothing to fault her on. The fury he'd once felt was forgotten. She was kind and gentle, and, in her innocence, sexy as hell.

He turned quickly back to the sink, but her image remained: soft wisps of pecan-colored hair framing her face; warm, amber eyes; delicate shoulders; gentle breasts. A heat rose in his body with stunning speed. Bowing his head, he gritted his teeth against it.

That was when her voice came to him softly, almost timidly. "What time shall I be ready tomorrow?"

It was a minute before he could relax his jaw, and then he wasn't sure if the tension in his voice was sexual or not. She still hadn't said if she'd return with him. "I'll wake you." He heard her slide back her chair and get up. "Karen?" Turning, he found her with her hand on the jamb and her back to him. "Will you be coming back with me?"

An hour or two before, she'd probably have refused him. One part of her would have regretted it, but she'd have felt she was doing the right thing. Now, she wasn't sure what the right thing was. Brice didn't seem the grump he once had. Oh, yes, he still had his moods, but with each tidbit she picked up about the man behind the moods, she became more and more intrigued. He was a puzzle; she had a handful of pieces, but she wanted the rest. There was only one way to get them.

Bowing her head, she whispered, "Yes. I'll be coming back with you." Then she left the room before she had second thoughts.

7

Ithaca was pitch black when a hand on Karen's shoulder shook her awake. She opened an eye, then flipped over in fright to look up into Brice's shadowed face. The only light was that which spilled in from the hall and silhouetted his large, looming form.

"Time to get up," he said.

She couldn't imagine why, at first. Though her fright quickly passed, it was a minute before her mind began to function. "What time is it?"

"Six. I have to be back at the hospital by nine."

She immediately pushed herself up. "Okay. I'll be ready."

"Your pill's in the bathroom. Ten minutes?"

She nodded and was swinging her feet to the floor as he left. She looked up in time to see him clear the door and disappear. He was wearing a running suit. She wondered whether that was what he planned to wear in the car, then wondered what *she* planned to wear in the car. She turned the light on and was in the process of contemplating that when Brice returned.

In two strides he was across the floor, placing a fleecy bundle in her arms. "Sweat suit. Warm and comfortable." He was back at the door in another two strides, but there he paused. Without turning, he said, "Your own clothes are in the hall closet downstairs. If you'd rather wear those—"

"These will be fine," Karen said.

He hesitated, nodded, then was gone.

Ten minutes later, he stood in the front hall watching Karen come down the stairs. His gaze slipped over her body. She looked adorable; he didn't know whether to laugh or cry. Reluctant to do either, he said, "You look like a deflated chipmunk."

She *felt* like a deflated chipmunk, because Brice looked like anything but. In those ten minutes he had somehow managed to shower, shave and toss on a shirt, sweater and cords. He looked fresh and ready to face the day in style.

Karen, too, had showered, but she didn't feel as fresh and ready as he looked. She knew that had something to do with her illness; she still felt weak and, because she was sleeping so soundly, a little hung over. She had to believe that she'd feel better— more herself psychologically—once she got some of her own things from home.

Not that she minded the feel of Brice's sweat suit. The fact that at some point he'd worn it himself made her feel all warm inside.

Averting her gaze, she spotted her boots by the closet door. She took them to the stairs, sat on the third step and pulled them on over the wool socks Brice had enclosed—along with her underwear—in the sweat suit. Returning, she let him help her on with her coat.

With a hand at her back, he ushered her through the kitchen and into the garage. His black BMW stood there, slightly spattered from the weather's recent inclemency. Beside it, looking less spattered but more battered, was her Chevy.

Coming to a halt at the BMW's nose, Brice trained his eyes on the Chevy and asked, "Do you want to take your car?"

Karen understood that he was giving her a last chance to change her mind about returning, and while she had no intention of doing so, she appreciated the gesture. "My heating system is lousy."

"I had it fixed."

"Oh."

"So?"

She thought for a minute, then wrinkled up her nose. "Nah. The windshield wipers are broken."

"Not anymore."

"You didn't fix the radio, too, did you? I'm not a listener, which is why I didn't care whether it worked or not. I hope you didn't spend money on *that*—"

"No. I didn't feel there was a safety factor involved."

Karen bit her lip. The accusation was subtle, but it was there. She looked sharply at Brice, prepared to defend herself, if need be. But he wasn't looking at her. He was looking in the opposite direction, awaiting her answer.

"No, I don't want to take my car," she said with spirit. "I like yours better." And with that, she went straight to the passenger's side, opened the door and slid in.

The drive was a quiet one. Once Karen settled down after that little rise, she relaxed and found that she *did* like Brice's car better than hers. The seats were more plush, the ride silent and smooth. Given the lack of traffic at that early hour, they made good time. The day was dawning gray and cool when they pulled up at the wood frame house in Syracuse that Karen called home.

For the first time, looking at it as Brice would see it, the shabbiness of the place hit her. As she led him to the door at the back that led to the stairs that led to her third-floor apartment, she was thinking that the house badly needed a paint job. Actually, she decided as she pulled and tugged, pulled and tugged until the door finally opened, the house needed more than a paint job.

The three flights were long and narrow. She was visibly winded by the time they reached the top and she'd opened the door to her apartment.

"Sit," Brice instructed.

The instruction was unnecessary. Karen was already en route to the desk chair. The instant she reached it, she sank gratefully onto its canvas sling.

Hands buried in the pockets of his cords so that they pushed his topcoat aside, Brice looked around the room. The apartment was, in fact, a garret, though somehow that designation made it sound more luxurious than it was. It was an attic. A bathroom had been built at one end, and a small kitchenette stood

at the other, but it was still an attic—doubtlessly con-
verted for the sake of the rent.

Brice turned, then turned again.

"Pretty bad, huh?" Karen said self-consciously.

It was pretty bad, but he didn't say so. He'd decided to make an attempt to be less abrasive. It was
going to take some effort; old habits died hard. He'd
nearly blown it with the deflated chipmunk comment,
though she hadn't taken offense at that. But he
thought he'd done quite well in not calling her car a
rattletrap, and he was determined to keep his opinion
of her apartment to himself.

Actually, the more he looked, the less bad it did
look. True, the rafters were water-stained and warped
and had nails sticking out every which way in odd
places. The floor was covered with vintage linoleum
that curled at the edges. The sink was ancient, the
stove even worse.

But the place was clean. The walls were painted
white, and the miscellaneous pieces of furniture and
their coverings—a comforter on the bed, café curtains
on the windows, a recycled dresser, nightstand and
desk, the deck chair she sat in—were all of bright and
varied colors. Brice guessed that Karen had spent
many a free hour painting when she'd first moved in.
She'd come close to creating a rainbow.

"Not bad," he said and glanced at her. She was
wrapped in her coat, seeming chilled. He looked for
a thermostat, found none, then spotted a radiator and
within seconds was trying to twist its knob.

"It's on," Karen said quickly. "When I left on

Friday, I had no idea I wouldn't be back, and since I wasn't feeling great, I wanted the place to stay warm. If I turn off the heat for even a few hours, the temperature in here drops something awful.''

Forgetting his resolution, Brice growled, ''The temperature in here is something awful even with it on. Is this the best your landlord can do?''

''I guess so.''

''What do you mean, 'you guess so'? Haven't you told him you're cold?''

She raised one shoulder and huddled into it. ''I asked him if the radiator was working, and he said it was. That was last December, when it was really cold. It's not so bad now. If I've made it through this far, I'll make it to spring.''

''You nearly didn't make it,'' Brice pointed out with a scowl. ''If you'd had proper heat in here, you might not have been as sick. I have a mind to report this place to the board of health.''

Karen straightened in her seat. ''If you do that,'' she said quietly, looking him in the eye, ''the landlord will fix the radiator and raise the rent to compensate, and I won't be able to afford it, so I'll have to move. Please don't, Brice.''

The sheer quiet of her voice was a powerful plea. Brice stared at her for a minute, then raised both palms in a hands-off gesture. By the time he dropped his hands, she'd risen from the chair and was on her knees, tugging a large duffel bag from under the bed.

Brice hauled her unceremoniously back to her feet. ''What are you doing?''

"Getting something to put clothes into."

"You're not supposed to be working. What do you think I'm here for?"

"To drive me back and forth."

"To help you pack."

"But you don't know where things are."

"So tell me." Bending from the waist, he swept the bag onto the bed. "Now, sit." He pointed to a spot by the duffel bag and waited until she'd complied, then he opened the bag wide and rubbed his hands together.

Karen didn't appreciate being treated like a dim-witted child. She decided that she was just offended enough, just defiant enough, just rubber-kneed enough to sit like a queen and give orders. So, crossing one leg over the other, she pointed to the closet. "Open the door." He did. "I want the sneakers and the black flats. They're on the floor beside the sewing machine."

"I can see where they are."

"Put them at the bottom of the bag. They're the heaviest."

He gave her a look as he carried the footwear to the bed. "I've packed bags before."

"That's good," she said brightly and waited until he'd stowed the shoes. "Now go back to the closet and get my jeans." He retraced his steps. "There are two pairs on hangers—" she watched him run a seeking hand along the edge of her clothes "—no, not those—there, that's right—and the ones beside them.'' He started back toward the bed. "Oh, wait—my belt—it's on the hook at the side.''

"You don't need a belt with jeans.''

"I do if I want to blouse up a sweater.''

He recalled the comment she'd made about being able to take unnotable clothing and make it notable, and without further question he went back for the belt. When it had been stowed beside the jeans, Karen sent him back to the closet for sweaters.

"They're up on those shelves—see them?'' He put a hand to the proper spot. "Take the gray one on the bottom, the brown one above it and the cream one in the next pile.''

Each was large and heavy. Stacking them in his arms, Brice returned to the bag. There, holding them, he frowned at Karen. "Why gray, brown and cream?'' He looked at the two sweaters left on the shelf; they were black and white. "Why not red, green or blue?''

"I don't have any sweaters in those colors.''

"But why not? You obviously like those colors. Look at this place.''

Quite unnecessarily, she looked around. Her eyes were still on the dresser, which was a rich moss green with white trim, when she answered. "This place is for me. No one sees it, so I can go a little wild with the colors. My wardrobe is something else. I like to buy a few things of high quality, but if I do that, unless I want to wear the same two or three outfits over and over again, everything has to blend so I can mix and match. That means sticking to neutral colors.''

Brice was remembering how pretty she'd looked in the red robe he'd bought her, when she snapped her fingers, pointed to the sweaters he held, then to the duffel.

''I'll need turtlenecks, too. They're—''

''Hold it.'' He was spreading the sweaters over the jeans, trying to even out their bulk. ''Turtlenecks? Under these? You'll *roast* in my house.''

He had a point. ''Mmm, maybe you should forget the turtlenecks. How about a few blouses?'' He started back toward the closet. ''No, I'd really prefer the turtlenecks. They're more comfortable.'' He turned. She pointed toward the dresser. He headed that way. ''Then again, I would be awfully warm.'' He stopped, put his hands on his hips and glared. She held her breath for a minute before offering a contrite, ''Then again, a turtleneck may be good to wear alone. I think I should take a few. Third drawer down in the dresser.''

Brice removed three knit turtlenecks in muted shades from the drawer and added them to the fast filling duffel. But by then, she'd remembered that she needed a skirt or two.

''For what?'' he demanded.

''Classes.''

''I thought most college kids wore jeans.''

''I'm a little older than most college kids. Sometimes I like wearing skirts. And I always wear skirts when I visit Rowena,'' she added with the slight uptilt of her chin. "Are you going to give me trouble about that?"

"Give you trouble? Hah! You don't know what I've been getting from Rowena. She doesn't give a damn how I am, only how you are. She doesn't believe me when I say that you're better. You're right— you're not contagious anymore. So be my guest. Go see her."

Karen smiled broadly. "Thank you."

Brice stood utterly motionless for a minute. He didn't understand how a simple smile could take his breath away, but Karen's smiles did. They lit her face, then his insides. It had happened enough times now for him to know the feeling, but rather than growing used to it, he felt harder hit each time.

She should only know the power she held, he mused. She should only know what he'd do for that smile.

Turning toward the closet, he said gruffly, "Tell me which skirts." She did. They were soon packed. "Now what?"

While he'd been doing the skirts, his dark head bent over the duffel bag, she'd been debating. By rights, she should tell him that the rest was personal. But she didn't want to. He'd been so overbearing when he'd told her to sit and let him work that she figured she ought to do just that. There was, of course, the issue of her own self-consciousness. But she figured she could overcome that. Watching the big man handle the little things would be worth it.

"Second drawer of the dresser," she said.

Brice opened it and found himself confronting a wild assortment of panty hose. Inhaling sharply at the oddly erotic sight, he caught a wisp of jasmine. "Swell," he muttered, gritting his teeth.

"Hmmm?"

"What happened in here?"

Envisioning the invasion of some form of pest, Karen slid from the bed and ran to the dresser. "What do you mean?"

"It's a mess!"

She looked into the drawer. She looked up at Brice. "It looks fine to me."

"It's a mess!"

"You just said that, but what do you expect with things like these?" Dipping a finger into the drawer, she hooked a pair of sheer somethings and held them up. "Have you ever tried neatly arranging legs like these?"

"Of course, I haven't. I don't wear stockings."

"Ahh."

"Karen…"

"They slither all over the place, Brice. There's no good way to fold them that stays. It's just easiest dropping everything in the drawer." Which was exactly what she did with what she'd hooked. Then she returned to the bed.

Brice toyed with the idea of letting her take over, but there was something of a challenge in the way she'd flounced away. She didn't think he could do it. Well, she was wrong. "Which of these…things do you want?"

She was sitting with deliberate primness, hands folded in her lap. "Just grab two or three. There are some wool ones farther back in the drawer. I'll need two or three of those, and several pairs of knee socks. They should be by the wool tights."

Pulling one pair of panty hose from the mess, Brice drew it up until its legs came free, then did the same with a second pair and a third. He felt like he was serving spaghetti—only spaghetti had never stirred his libido the way the touch of Karen's nylons was doing. With a less steady hand, he grabbed some wool tights and several pairs of knee socks. Returning to the bed, he quickly deposited them in the bag.

Karen was entranced, then emboldened by the color that had stolen to his cheeks. "Now the top drawer," she instructed.

Even before opening the drawer, Brice knew what he would find. She had to wear something beneath her clothes. The problem was that he'd already had a glimpse of her underthings—neatly folded, after they'd been washed by Meg—and that glimpse hadn't helped. He'd initially pegged Karen as the plain cotton panty type. She wasn't.

Before him was a sweet gathering of nylon and lace. Pressing his lips together hard, he tried to convince himself that he was at the lingerie counter of a department store. It didn't work. This was Karen's drawer. Each of the things in it she'd worn—not only worn, but worn intimately.

"Any problem, Brice?" she asked innocently.

He shot a glance at her through the mirror. If it

hadn't been for that innocent tone, he mightn't have thought twice about the innocence of her expression. But the two together were a bit much. It suddenly struck him that she was enjoying herself.

"No problem," he said with a revival of control. Holding her gaze, he asked, "How many pairs of panties should I pack?"

"They don't take up much room. How about six or seven?"

With a sage nod—and traitorously shaky hands— he took the panties from the drawer.

"Uh…wait," she burst out. "You didn't take the fuchsia ones, did you? They're not really practical. They're cut too high, so they're uncomfortable with clothes of a rougher fabric, like jeans."

Brice thumbed through the pile of panties until he touched on the fuchsia ones. Removing them, he replaced them with a pale pink pair. He liked pale pink. It was feminine and sweet. Set under a robe that was red and hot, it was dynamite.

Blotting his damp upper lip with the back of his hand, he forced himself on. "And bras?"

In any other situation she would have blushed and said, "I'll take care of those." But she was rather enjoying his discomfort. So she asked, "What have I got there?"

For just a minute he lost his composure. "What do you mean—'what have I got there'? You've got *bras* here."

"How many?"

"How the hell do I know?"

"If you count them," she said sweetly, "I'll know how many to take. I think I have six in all, but I'm wearing one, and another one is probably in the laundry bag in the bathroom. I'd like to leave a clean one here so I'll have it when I get back."

Brice took a slow, calming breath, then one by one counted the bras in the drawer. "Five here."

"Five?" She frowned. "That would make seven in all. I didn't think I had seven.... Oh," she brightened, "I know, you must have counted the strapless one. Is there a strapless one there?"

Brice took a second slow, calming breath, then one by one sorted through the bras in the drawer. His control was being tried. There was something incendiary about dealing with bras that had at one point or another been filled with the breasts of the woman behind him. He didn't know whether it was better or worse that he'd never actually seen those breasts. He'd seen vague curves, but that didn't count. Once he'd come close to touching them—when he'd listened to her heart—but she'd been so sick then that the last thing on his mind had been her body. It wasn't the last thing on his mind now.

"Yes," he said in a voice that was beginning to fray at the edges, "there's a strapless one here."

"Well, I don't need it. I really only use it in the summer when I'm wearing a tank top or a halter dress, but I won't have use for anything like that in this weather. Put the strapless one aside. How many does that leave?"

"You know how many," he gritted under his breath.

"Hmm?"

"Four."

"Okay, take three and leave the other. That should do it." Feeling a certain amount of pleasure at the sight of this tall, oft-arrogant man doing her bidding, she watched his bowed head in the mirror as he replaced the strapless bra in the drawer. He was halfway between the dresser and the bed when she said, "Maybe I should leave the blue one here." He stopped. "I'm not sure I'd use it. The softer colors are more practical." He started back toward the dresser. "No...wait...bring it here for a minute."

As he returned, she took in the ruddiness of his complexion. She liked that added color. It made him look younger, more vulnerable. She liked to think of him as vulnerable because somehow that evened the tables a little. If he was uncomfortable handling her things, tough. He'd asked for it. He'd *insisted*. Any discomfort he felt was his due.

Dropping her gaze to the bra, she retrieved the blue panties from the bag, and held the two side by side. She slid the fabric between her fingers, comparing the color and the lace. "They do look nice together. Maybe I should take them as a set. What do you think?"

Brice was thinking that with the sensual swirl of silky stuff between her fingers, he'd reached his limit. Head still lowered toward the duffel, he raised his eyes to Karen's. "I think," he said in a deep, sandy rumble, "that this has gone on long enough."

Karen felt a moment's unsureness. He didn't look as awkward as she'd thought moments before. "What do you mean?"

"I mean," he said, "that the game is over. You've worn it out."

"What game?" she asked, thinking that while he didn't look exactly angry, he didn't look thrilled. He was somewhere in between, only she couldn't quite put her finger on the spot.

"I think you know," he said as he lowered his hands to the bed on either side of her hips. She leaned back to give him room, but he simply walked forward with his hands, crowding her, crowding her, until she'd leaned so far back that she lay on the bed. "You can't play with a man that way, Karen."

"I didn't mean—"

"Yes, you did. You meant to taunt me, only I'm not sure you knew the consequences of that." His hands were by her shoulders, thumbs sliding beneath.

"But you were the one who told me to sit and let you work," she argued meekly. She was beginning to identify the spot between angry and thrilled where Brice was. She was beginning to wonder if she'd indeed gone a little too far.

"I meant what I said," he claimed. "I wanted you to rest. So what did you do? You sat there like a little Hitler giving orders."

"Don't you like taking orders?" she asked with a

spurt of indignance. "Think of how *I've* felt these past few days."

Brice's voice came to her on a low, husky wave. "I don't mind taking orders. I had no trouble when it came to your shoes and jeans and skirts and sweaters. When we got to the frills and lace, that was something else."

Belatedly, she felt a touch of remorse. "You should have told me you didn't want to do that part."

"I would have been fine doing that part if you hadn't made a major production of it." He threw his voice up an octave in imitation of hers. "How many panties do I have in the drawer, Brice? Count them, Brice. I don't *want* the fuchsia ones, Brice, they're cut too high. Maybe I should leave the blue bra here—oh, but it goes with the blue panties." His voice fell. "Do you think I'm totally insensitive?"

"Of course, not."

"I'm not made of stone."

"Sometimes you seem it," she bit off rashly.

He pressed his lower legs more firmly into the side of the bed, in the process forcing hers apart. "Well, I'm not. I'm flesh and blood. I have the same urges other men have. Have you forgotten last night so fast?"

That kiss. She'd tried not to think about it. She'd tried not to think about the powerful things it had stirred up inside her. But trying was one thing, doing another. No, she hadn't forgotten that kiss. And as for the things it had stirred up, she remembered them vividly. Remembered…and felt. Brice was very close, very large, very masculine.

"Did you think that was an aberration?" he asked. "Did you think I did it for kicks?"

"No."

"Didn't it occur to you that if I kissed you, it was because I found you attractive?"

"I…I didn't think about that."

"Why not?"

"I was sick. I didn't feel attractive. I'm not used to thinking of myself as attractive."

Brice supposed he could buy that. She said that she wasn't involved with a man and hadn't been for a long while. He knew that between school and work she was overextended. She barely had time to think of men, or sex, or attraction.

"Then why the underwear?" he asked.

She didn't know what he meant. "Don't most people wear it?"

"Not sexy stuff. Not stuff in colors like those. Not stuff that slips through your hand like a sigh. If you're on such a tight budget, how in the hell can you afford stuff like that?"

"I buy on sale," she murmured.

"But why things like that? They're out of step with the rest of your clothes. Looking at you when you're dressed, a person would never dream you had those underneath."

He was close, coming more so by fractions of an inch. She took a quick breath and whispered, "They're for me."

"They make you feel good?"

"Yes."

"Which means," he said in a husky voice, "that beneath the sedate facade of a hard-working college student is a siren."

Eyes fixed on his mouth, she gave a convulsive swallow. "No siren."

His answer was a heated visual exploration of her face.

"Brice..."

Lowering his head the few necessary inches, he took her mouth. She tried to turn her head away, but he framed her chin with his hand as he'd done the last time and whispered against her lips, "Shhhh." She twisted again. "Shhhh." He held her firmly. His tongue touched her lower lip in a single dab before he opened his mouth and gave her an ardent caress. He stroked her. He moved his mouth as though hers were a piece of clay that needed warmth, moisture and kneading to come alive.

In short seconds, Karen was back to the intense level of feeling that had frightened her the night before. "Um-um," she protested in a closed-mouth appeal and opened her hands against his arms to lever him away.

Brice eased up. He wanted to excite her, not frighten her. He wanted to turn her on and see if she felt what he did. He'd left their last kiss hungry, and the hunger had worsened each time he'd allowed himself to remember her taste. He wanted to taste her again, but even more than that, he wanted her to know the hunger.

So he slid his mouth over hers, back and forth, then from a new angle, creating a friction that was light and sensual. Giving her more space, he abandoned her mouth for her cheek, pressing slow, open pecks there that were deceptively lazy.

Karen was horrified. The more gentle he was, the more he stirred her. "Brice, please," she whispered. Her hands exerted pressure to keep his upper torso off her, but the weight of his hips pressed her into the bed. He felt good against her—too good. She squirmed to dislodge him, but his body grew more rigid.

"Don't," he commanded, raising his head for a minute. His voice was hoarse, his eyes dark, sensually alive as he looked down at her. He struggled to gentle his tone, but still it sounded sandy. "I won't hurt you."

Her eyes were wide. "I know...but I don't want this."

"Don't want what?"

Her cheeks grew pinker. "This."

"My kissing you? Am I that awful a kisser?"

"No."

"Was it so bad just now?"

"No, but—"

"But what?"

She sent him a pleading look that said, "You make me feel all hot and achy inside." For the life of her, though, she couldn't say the words aloud.

She didn't have to. Brice read them in her amber eyes. His own widened and went even darker. "It felt good?" he asked in a rasping whisper.

She nodded. "But it isn't right."

"Who says so?"

"Me."

"What about me?"

"You're a man. You want a body. Anyone would do."

Brice felt a spurt of anger. "Is that what you think?"

She hesitated. "Isn't it true?"

"No."

"Then why me? I'm not soft and curvy. And I'm not a siren."

"So says you."

Unable to buy his implication, she squeezed her eyes shut. But Brice only took that opportunity to kiss those eyes, first one, then the other in leisurely succession. His mouth moved to her forehead, then the bridge of her nose, then her chin. He discovered that each of those spots was as sweet-tasting as her mouth.

In the wake of his kisses, a heady warmth spread through Karen's veins. No longer squeezed shut, her eyes were no more than lightly closed. Her will to resist dwindled. She felt a little high.

When his mouth touched hers this time, she didn't fight. She didn't have time, because the touch was there, then gone, there, then gone. It moved over her face again, a magnificent monarch butterfly alighting and taking off in a pattern only it knew—a pattern, she decided after a minute or two, that was designed to drive her mad.

"Brice, don't," she breathed.

"Don't what?"

"Tease. It hurts."

Brice pulled himself out of a daze to look at her. Her eyes were half-lidded, her cheeks flushed, her lips parted. It was another minute before he realized what she meant. Then it was his body that responded first, by tightening reflexively. When his mind caught up, passion's kindling burst into flame.

Holding his weight on his forearms, he slid his fingers into her hair and captured her mouth in a kiss that was like none he'd given her before. This one was deep and thorough. It nudged her lips open and sent his tongue into the dark interior from which he'd previously been barred. The kiss was hot and wet— and it wasn't one-sided. Karen was kissing him back with a sweet, hungry need.

Moaning, he moved his body against hers. And she didn't complain. She needed the friction, too. Those hands that had once held him off were now clutching the dark wool of his topcoat. She didn't know if she was holding him to her or simply holding on, but it didn't matter. She felt positively drugged.

Releasing her lips, he whispered her name in a voice rough with need. The heat of his body penetrated her clothing. The smokiness of his eyes clouded hers.

"Let me touch," he whispered, and before she could think to demur he was pushing her coat aside, spanning her waist with a hand, moving upward. When he touched her breast, she made a soft, involuntary sound. She closed her eyes; her head drifted to the side. She felt his fingers spreading over her softness, moving from one side to the other and up and down as though to create a visual image from something as yet only tactile.

It felt divine. He molded his fingers to her breast, molded her breast to his fingers, and though his touch was firm, he didn't hurt her. Any pain she felt was from the gathering coil at the pit of her stomach. She was momentarily distracted from that when he scraped the tip of one finger over her tightly budded nipple. With a tiny cry, she opened her eyes.

"What?" he coaxed in a husky whisper. He continued to stroke her.

Covering his hand with her own, she stilled its movement. He waited for her to remove his hand, but she simply pressed it harder to her breast. As she did, she closed her eyes and arched her back.

Brice took one labored breath, then another. He had wanted to stay in control, had wanted to concentrate on arousing her, but she was already aroused, and seeing that, he couldn't hold back any longer. His mouth came down hard on hers, demanding an even deeper response than it had before. He received that response and more.

Abandoning his coat, Karen dug her fingers into his hair and held him close, while her tongue played with his. She had no idea what she was doing; it was all instinct and desire. But the results were so heavenly that she kept at it, and when she felt Brice's hand slip under the hem of her sweatshirt, climb again, then find her silk-covered breast, she felt a wave of relief.

Her skin was hot, and for a brief instant Brice wondered if the heat were from illness. Dragging his mouth from hers, he raised his head and captured her gaze. "Okay?" he whispered in an uneven breath.

She gave a tiny, quick nod. Her breathing was shallow, a little raspy, but her color was better than good. Her cheeks were a soft pink, her lips rouged. She ran her tongue along the lower one. She dropped her hands to his neck. She eyed him expectantly, waiting for him to move the hand that covered her bra.

For Brice, the anticipation was nearly as precious as what he finally found when he curled his fingers under the lace edging and peeled it back. He pictured it as he felt it, that small, hard nub popping free and straining toward his flesh. He touched it with the tip of his finger, then slid that same fingertip back and forth across the sensitive peak.

Karen gave a sharp cry and sucked in her breath— then broke into a harsh, hacking cough. Frightened, Brice forgot his own need. Withdrawing his hand, he pulled her to a seated position and rubbed her back until she'd caught her breath.

"Oh God," she whispered, trembling as she buried her face against his neck.

Not particularly steady himself, he folded her in his arms and he held her close. "Shhh."

"I'm sorry."

"It's okay." He paused for several short breaths. "Was it good?"

She nodded.

Feeling the movement, he closed his eyes and thought about how right she felt in his arms.

After a minute, her muffled voice came to him. "I didn't cough on purpose."

"I know."

"I'm not a tease."

"I know."

"Or a siren."

He said nothing to that, because though he was sure she didn't do it on purpose, she was seductive as hell. It wasn't a physical thing, though he thought she was beautiful. Her body was a dozen turn-ons—from her hair to her shoulders and breasts and hips. But the real seduction came from inside—from her innocence, from the quiet of her voice, her unpretentiousness. It also came from the fact that she had no intention of getting involved. That somehow made things different. She had no intention of getting involved, yet the sweet sounds that had come from her throat said she *was* involved, and that made him feel special. It made him feel as though he were the only man in the world who could please her, and that made him feel whole for the first time in his life.

Given the implications, he was deeply shaken.

8

For several minutes longer, Brice continued to hold Karen, but not in passion. That had passed in part when she'd started to cough, in part when he'd realized that she had the potential for knocking him on his ear. He wasn't head over heels in love, but the seeds were there. He hadn't felt as touched by a woman since…no, he'd *never* felt it before.

His marriage had been a deliberately planned undertaking, lacking both spontaneity and passion. He'd thought himself in love because the timing was right. After the relationship had quietly folded, he'd decided that he didn't really know what love was.

Now he was beginning to get glimpses of something so rich and deep that, if it was love, it put all past impressions to shame. Those glimpses frightened him. He was frightened that they wouldn't prove to be real; then again, he was frightened that they would, and that he'd somehow blow it. He didn't have a good track record when it came to interpersonal relations. He'd never been comfortable with his peers and, aside from his marriage, had never dated any one woman for long. A relationship with Karen would be paving new ground. He suddenly felt that there was a whole lot at stake.

Gently, he released her. Quietly and a little humbly, he rose from the bed to resume packing. Without looking at her, he suggested that she see to her toiletries.

More than a little unsure, herself, Karen was grateful for an excuse to escape into the bathroom for a minute. Her insides still quivered—and not from coughing. If Brice's first kiss had been a nine on a scale from one to ten, this one had been a fourteen. No, she amended, it had entered a whole new range; it wasn't in the same category as that first kiss at all.

The first time around she hadn't participated. This time she had, and it had been wonderful—wonderful, but not nearly enough. She was in a state of suspended desire. She was frustrated. And that was a new experience for her.

One by one, she gathered toiletries in the crook of her arm, then returned to deposit them in the duffel bag. Brice was at the window with his back to her, all broad shoulders and straight, lean hips. She wondered what he was thinking, whether he was regretting the kiss, or whether he was wanting more. He was a healthy male. She knew that he'd been aroused; she'd felt the strength of him against her, had heard his rough breathing, had seen the heat in his eyes. Oh yes, he'd been aroused, but whether that pleased him was another story.

Crossing to the desk, she busied herself loading texts, papers and notebooks into a book bag. Only when she had everything she felt she'd need did she zip the bag and turn to Brice. He was waiting, wearing a thoroughly uncharacteristic look of confusion. After studying her for a minute, he blinked, and the expression vanished.

"All set?" he asked in a mellow tone.

She nodded.

Slinging the duffel bag strap over one shoulder and her book bag over the other, he motioned her to the door.

Disoriented most aptly described how Brice felt through the rest of that day. He dropped Karen back at the house, went to the hospital, returned to the house and saw patients until late in the afternoon, so it wasn't a case of his having nothing to occupy his mind. He was for the most part on familiar turf. Only when he thought of Karen did he feel upended.

Karen, meanwhile, was diverting her own mind by visiting Rowena, who greeted her with a skewed smile and the longest stream of words Karen had ever heard from her.

"You're all...r-r-right! I was worried. Brice doesn't like me t-t-to worry...b-b-but I didn't know if I could believe him when he...s-s-said you were better. Y-y-you looked so sick last Friday."

"I was," Karen said with a wry smile. The smile warmed. "I'm better now."

Rowena's gaze homed in on that smile. "Tell me...w-w-what happened Friday."

Feeling somewhat cavalier with that part of it over, Karen told her about passing out in the snow and being scooped up by Brice. She told of how she'd been out of it when she'd first arrived at his house and how she'd slept through most of the weekend.

"How was...B-B-Brice?"

"He was fine."

"He isn't s-s-social."

"I wasn't looking for social. All I wanted was a warm place to lie down. He gave me that, plus medicine and hot tea."

Rowena's wrinkled mouth puckered even more. "I hate tea."

Karen nearly laughed at the older woman's expression of distaste. "Me, too. But it was hot, and it helped. Brice knew what he was doing when he brought it."

"Kind?"

"Was he?" Karen asked in clarification, then nodded.

"The t-t-truth," Rowena demanded, eyes chiding.

"He was very kind."

"Always?"

"Whenever I needed him, he was there for me."

"Karen..."

Karen took the old woman's gnarled hand and said softly but with force, "He really was good, Rowena. He has his moods. He can be curt, even rude. But he took care of me. You can be proud of him."

Rowena seemed only marginally satisfied with that. Wanting to please her, Karen added, "I'm going to be staying at his house for a while. He's convinced that the only way I'll get the rest I need is if he supervises my convalescence. I thought the idea was absurd at first, but he has it all worked out.''

She told of the leaves of absence he'd arranged for her from her jobs. ''He's even contacted a fellow to drive me to Syracuse and back when I have classes. Apparently the man is unemployed, his two sons are patients of Brice's and he can't pay the bills. That doesn't bother Brice, but it bothers this man. Brice thought that giving him something to do in exchange for his children's medical treatment would offer him a measure of dignity. I agree.''

Rowena was looking more and more satisfied. ''You...l-l-like him.''

''Who? Brice?''

Rowena's eyes said, ''Who else?'' in a smug kind of way.

''I respect him,'' Karen said.

''Like him,'' Rowena insisted.

Karen didn't have to think about whether she did, just whether she should admit it. Whatever existed between Brice and her could disintegrate any day in a spate of angry words. It wouldn't do for Rowena to get her hopes up.

She went with a gentle version of the truth. ''Yes, I like him. But that doesn't mean there's more. Brice has his life, I have mine. We're both loners. Neither of us is used to living with someone.''

''You can...g-g-get used to it.''

''Maybe, but Brice can be difficult. I don't know if I want to get used to that.''

''He needs you.''

"He may need a woman. I'm not at all sure he needs me. I remind him of unhappy things."

"Like the accident?"

Karen nodded. "He looks at me and remembers that it was my car that hit you."

"Maybe once. No...m-m-more."

"How do you know?"

"His...v-v-voice." When Karen shook her head in denial of that, Rowena asked, "Why did you agree to...s-s-stay with him?"

Karen gave a one-shouldered shrug. "I don't know. Maybe because I love the house."

Rowena's lips thinned.

"It's a beautiful house," Karen rushed on in an attempt to give merit to the argument. "It's large and warm. Brice keeps the living room fire going. I've never been as comfortable anywhere."

Rowena said a very quiet, "No," so Karen tried again.

"Meg is there. It's nice to know I'm not alone."

"Maybe."

"Maybe Brice is right. I need a rest. If I were at my own place, I'd spend all my time studying. He won't let me do that."

"Good."

A harried look crept to Karen's eyes. "I don't know about that. I'm already behind in my work."

"You'll g-g-get it done."

The harried look began to dissipate. "That's what Brice says. He says it's a matter of pacing, that since

I won't be working I'll be able to get everything done without killing myself.''

"He w-w-wants you there.''

"He's taking the role of healer seriously.''

"He *w-w-wants* you there.''

"It's a big house. He can come and go without seeing me.''

"He won't. He wants to…s-s-see you.''

"But how can he want me there when he doesn't have you there?'' Karen asked. Seconds after the words left her mouth, she regretted them, but they'd been hovering at the back of her mind for too long. They'd had to come out sooner or later.

Rowena didn't appear the least bit fazed. To the contrary, she seemed to straighten in her chair. "He doesn't have me there…b-b-because I won't *be* there.''

Karen was taken aback. "You mean, he's asked?''

"Asked, demanded, ranted and raved…he wanted me to live with him b-b-before the accident. I refused then. I feel s-s-stronger about it now. If I were in… B-B-Brice's home, I'd be lonely. Here I have friends.''

"But he's family,'' Karen argued and quickly felt the movement of Rowena's hand in hers.

"You feel that way because you have…n-n-no family. I do. Brice and now you.''

Karen held her hand tighter.

"I have the…m-m-money for this place. I won't be a burden to anyone.''

"You wouldn't be a burden.''

"Sweetly said. But daily care is d-d-daily care. I

have moods, too. The apple...d-d-doesn't fall far from the tree."

"I've never seen your moods."

"Brice has."

"Oh."

"B-b-besides, he needs to be lonely." When Karen frowned, Rowena took a breath and went on. "He has to know loneliness t-t-to know he doesn't want it. It's too easy for him to fall b-b-back on me. But I won't be around forever. And then where...w-w-will he be? He needs a wife and children. He loves children."

"So I guessed."

"So I know."

Karen couldn't help but grin at the quick reply. In turn Rowena couldn't help but comment on the grin. "You look...b-b-better. More relaxed. Happier."

Lowering her eyes to the hand that held Rowena's, Karen thought about that for a minute. "I do feel better," she admitted softly. "Not as oppressed." She raised her eyes to her friend's. "But it's wrong for me to be leaning on Brice like I am. Everything my life was before will start up again in less than a month. If I'm spoiled...."

"You won't be."

"I do wonder about it."

"Don't."

"But what happens if..."

Rowena's eyes pressed for completion of the sentence, but Karen couldn't finish. She'd been about to ask what would happen if she fell in love with Brice and he didn't return her love. But that wasn't Rowena's worry. It was Karen's…only Karen's.

Karen didn't allow herself to think about it after she left Rowena. She returned to the house and spent an hour rereading the notes from which she planned to write her history paper. To her subsequent chagrin, she fell asleep on the living room sofa, before a blazing fire, with the papers in her lap.

When she woke up, she found Brice in the kitchen slicing the pot roast Meg had cooked. "What can I do?" she asked.

He darted her a glance. "Want to set the table?"

"Sure." Going to the same cabinets and drawers she'd seen him go to the night before, she took out what they'd need, set everything on the table, then sank quietly into one of the chairs. Minutes later, Brice filled both plates with hearty servings of meat, potatoes and carrots, poured two glasses of milk and joined her.

It was a most surprising meal for Karen because it was peaceful from start to finish. Brice wanted to know how Rowena was; Karen told him, then told him about the article she'd read her about boat-building in Nantucket. "Rowena said she owned a boat once."

"She did. It was a sloop. We used to sail it off the coast of Maine. She had a place up there for a while."

"Did you spend a lot of time there with her?"

"Vacations and summers. My parents couldn't get away from the city for more than a week at a stretch, so Rowena made a point of being there for me. She thought it was important.'' His eyes had strayed toward the floor at the last but quickly returned to find Karen's. ''She hasn't had the boat for years. She sold it along with the house when she decided that she'd rather spend her vacations traveling than going to the same place over and over.''

''You were grown then?''

He nodded. ''And too busy to spend more than a few vacation days at a time anywhere.''

''Are you still?''

''I can be as busy as I want, but too busy is no good. I make time for vacations, now.''

Karen ate a little. Then, making innocent conversation, she said, ''Rowena's thinking of taking a cruise.'' As soon as she heard the words, she cringed inwardly and prepared herself for an outraged protest from Brice. It never came.

''She could do it,'' he stated calmly.

After a breath, Karen asked, ''Really?''

''With a companion, sure. Her condition isn't at or near any kind of crisis. She's making steady improvement. The best thing for her is to live. She'd probably love a cruise. She's the type.''

''Are you?''

Brice denied it at first. He claimed that he needed more action than a cruise had to offer. Then Karen started regurgitating some of the facts she'd picked up about cruises in the course of her reading, and Brice reconsidered. The kinds of cruises she described were a far cry from the stereotype. He didn't have to

ask if she would like to go on one of those offbeat
types of cruises. Enthusiasm sparkled in her eyes, her
voice, the animation of her face. And it was contagious. He found himself asking more and more, as
though she were a travel agent and he a potential
client. They were reveling in dream material, and it
was lovely.

Three hours—and much food, drink and conversation—had passed when Karen yawned. She
couldn't remember the last time she'd carried on such
a prolonged discussion with a single person. Brice,
too, seemed surprised when he looked at his watch.

Excusing herself when he wouldn't let her help
with the dishes, she retrieved her papers from the living room and went up to bed. Once again, she fell
asleep with the papers on her lap. When she awoke
the next morning, they were neatly piled on the
dresser along with a note, which read, ''If you'd like
to use a desk, help yourself to the one in my den. The
typewriter and word processor are in the records room
next door to that. Don't overdo it. I thought we'd go
out for dinner tonight.''

Karen's heart did a little two-step as she reread the
note. The prospect of going out to dinner with Brice
excited her. He'd been fun to be with the night before.

With something to look forward to, she had an easier time than she might have otherwise had applying
herself to the writing of her paper. Having completed
the research, she set right to work. She paused for a
break at noon to have lunch with Meg, and even allowing for a nap at midafternoon, she completed the

five-page piece and was in the process of typing it when Brice stopped by.

He stood over her shoulder, reading the few lines of the page she'd just typed. "Sounds interesting."

"Not really. Well, maybe it is, a little. There isn't too much leeway in freshman courses. I really wanted to address a different historical issue, but that one wasn't on the list of choices."

"The professor wouldn't make an exception for you?"

"Why should he?"

"Because you're older than the rest of the students and obviously taking this more seriously. Professors are skeptical of students who ask for substitute assignments in hopes of getting something easier. You wouldn't do that."

Gratified by his vote of confidence, Karen went back to her typing. But Brice remained at her shoulder. She was acutely aware of him, of the size of his body and its heat. And something else. With her sense of smell slowly returning, she was catching wisps of a most subtle scent. It came and went. She wasn't sure whether it was cologne, soap or simply clean male, but it intrigued her.

When she found herself superimposing Brice's image on the words she was to type, she lowered her hands to her lap and said softly, "I can't do this with you watching."

"Why not?"

"You make me nervous."

"Am I crowding you?"

"No. But you're *there.*"

"And you were never a Kelly Girl."

Karen's lips twitched at the corners. "Not quite."

"Why don't I have one of the girls type that? You've got everything written clear as day in long-hand. Any one of them could do it up in no time."

"You're not paying them to type my papers."

"No, but my receptionist spends a lot of time with a paperback novel in her lap. Am I paying her to read?"

"No."

"So she can type."

Karen looked up—way up—to meet his gaze. Once again that scent came to her. She felt a weird sensation in her knees and was grateful she was sitting. "Let me see how much I can get done on my own. It took me less time to write the paper than I'd expected, so I'm really ahead."

"But I want to go out to dinner."

He sounded so petulant that she couldn't hold back a smile. "Real hungry?"

"Yeah," Brice said in the hoarse voice her smile had given him. "The place I have in mind has great filet mignon. I can never get it to taste that way here."

Karen began to salivate. "Is this restaurant dressy? I didn't bring anything dressy."

"Your gray skirt and sweater would be just about right."

"Are you sure?"

"I'm sure."

They were perfect, she found. There were people

at the restaurant wearing everything from silk cocktail dresses to denim jumpsuits. What Brice had suggested put her right in the middle. Not only that, but he co-ordinated himself with her outfit by wearing a pair of gray slacks and a tweed blazer. She had to admit that with a crisp white shirt offsetting the healthy coloring of his skin and a paisley tie knotted neatly at his neck, he looked dashing. She was proud to be with him.

Brice was experiencing similar feelings. It wasn't often that he took women places in Ithaca. Most often in the past, when he'd felt need of female compan-ionship, he'd spent the weekend in Manhattan, where he was less likely to run into people he knew. He studiously avoided an Ithaca social life.

But he'd wanted to take Karen out. He'd wanted to see her dressed up, with her hair brushed out and flowing. He'd wanted to treat her to something she probably hadn't had much of before. It hadn't oc-curred to him that he'd reap a side benefit even as he walked with her to their table. He felt proud that she was with him, rather than with one of the other men in the room.

On the tails of those auspicious beginnings, dinner was as amicable an affair as it had been the evening before. Brice had his tongue under control. The only sharp word he offered was a pithy one, spoken early on and under his breath, directed at a couple whose son he had treated for various injuries not long before.

"That is probably the most frustrating part of my practice," he explained to Karen after he'd taken a healthy drink of his wine. "It's heartbreaking when a child comes in suffering from a serious illness. In the past year I've had kids with newly diagnosed cases of muscular dystrophy and cystic fibrosis. No one plans to get diseases like those; they just come. But when I see a child who's been battered—cruelly, unnecessarily, repeatedly—it's infuriating.''

Karen noted the hard set of his mouth and was grateful that this time around she hadn't caused it. ''Do you report the parents?''

''Sure. For whatever good it does. When the family has money and a reputation to protect, they'll do anything to keep child abuse from coming to light.'' He looked off in the direction of the pair in question. ''That particular family is one of the more prominent in the area. Well liked and professionally respected. They've been active at the university for years. Shortly after I reported a series of injuries with suspicious causes, I received a visit from their lawyer stating that if I dared breathe the slightest scandalous word again, I'd be slapped with a multimillion-dollar libel suit.''

''You didn't stop, did you?''

The determined expression he wore when he looked back at her added strength to his already rugged face. ''Are you kidding? I told the guy that if he wanted to talk blackmail, we could trot down to the local prosecutor's office, which was where—I told him—I intended to go anyway.''

''Did you?''

''Sure did.''

''What happened?''

Brice flipped his spoon over and back. Then he slowly raised his eyes to Karen's. "Last I heard, the case was dropped for lack of evidence. It'll be back in court, but only after that child suffers more."

Karen felt his frustration. "Will you see the child again?"

"I'd gladly see him again, but you can be sure the parents won't let me."

He grew quiet. His dark head was slightly bowed, eyes focused on the spoon as he turned it from side to side. She was watching him, thinking about dedication and frustration and how closely entwined they were, when the waiter arrived with their food.

It was an instant diversion. Karen, who had had a hint of things to come when the maître d' had spread her linen napkin on her lap, was delighted with the elegant presentation of the meal. Brice, who was more accustomed to fine restaurants than she, took pleasure in her pleasure—and when he took pleasure in something, he relaxed—and when he relaxed, he let down the defenses that kept him aloof.

He wanted to know about the courses she was taking. Helpless to resist, when she was being wined and dined so finely, she listed them, gave brief descriptions, answered his questions about requirements and electives. Then, when she'd finally stopped for a bite of her steak and a forkful of lyonnaise potatoes, he asked, "Did you originally plan to go to college in Syracuse, or did you choose it because of Rowena?"

The potatoes went down Karen's throat in a lump. She was surprised—not so much because he had asked, since she was used to his bluntness, but because he had asked in as innocent a manner. She studied his face, searched for signs of disdain and found none. What she did find were eyes that were warm and had less of a crease between them than usual, a nose that was straight but relaxed, a mouth that was very, very male. The tiny flick of a muscle at his jaw only added to the virile image.

Swallowing again, ostensibly to make sure the potatoes were down, she composed herself. "Up until five years ago, I lived with my family in Connecticut. After my mother died, I moved to New York to work, but living there wasn't as much fun as I'd imagined it would be. When it came to choosing a school, I thought I might like to try the South."

"Why the South?" Brice asked in a voice that was smooth and low.

"Because I'd never been there. I like going places I've never been, and I knew that it would only have to be for four years." She took a breath and went on as confidently as she could. "I'd been accepted at Emory, in Atlanta. After the accident, I decided to stay up here."

Brice echoed his earlier question. "Was it because of Rowena?" He meant no criticism. He was simply curious.

"Yes."

"Then why not Cornell? That's right here in town."

"I didn't get into Cornell. Syracuse gave me a scholarship."

Quietly finishing his steak, Brice thought about the disappointments she'd suffered in life. Everyone experienced disappointments; nobody made it through without some. But it seemed she'd had more than her share.

Cornell had no right to reject her, he decided. Next time they called *him* to address a child psych class, he'd think twice.

Oblivious to his thoughts, when her own were, strangely, on his hands as they manipulated his utensils, Karen ate, too. When she'd had as much as she could, she put down her fork, let out a breath and said, "Between Meg's cooking and meals like this, I think I've gained five pounds."

Brice hoped so. He examined her face with a tactile gaze. "They become you."

"But if I keep on at this rate, I'll be a blimp."

"No."

"I'm used to getting exercise. Back in Syracuse, I was on the go all the time. Waitressing is like a full night of aerobics."

"I'd rather you didn't do anything until you're better."

"I am better."

A muscle moved in his jaw, and he took a long, slow drink of water before he spoke. "I'll amend that, then. I'd rather you didn't do anything until you've taken the last of the penicillin. You've done a job on your body. It needs time to heal." Again he paused, this time wondering if he'd blown it with the comment about the job she'd done on her body. But she didn't seem upset. Maybe she was getting used to his manner. In a gruffer voice, he said, "When it's healed, you could run with me."

Karen's eyes lit up. "Run? You run? When?"

He caught his breath. Momentarily forgetting the serious issue of her health, he broke into a grin that was both amused and wry, "That's classic Rowena."

"What is?"

"What you just did—asking three questions in one breath. When something interested her, she wanted to know everything about it at once."

"Running fascinates me. How often do you go?"

"Every morning."

"From the house?"

He nodded.

"What time?"

"Early—six, sometimes five."

"That's why you were wearing a running suit when you woke me yesterday morning."

He nodded. "Do you run?"

She shrugged and gave a small, sheepish smile. "Nah."

"Why not?"

She thought about that for a minute. "I suppose I could say that I wouldn't feel safe running alone, but the truth is that I don't have the energy. I'm too tired in the morning and too tired at night, and I don't have the time during the day."

Again, a muscle moved in Brice's jaw. Karen realized that happened whenever he was holding in a retort. She rushed on.

"I know. You feel I'm doing too much, and maybe I am. But that's beside the point. Tell me about your running."

Wanting to avoid unpleasantness every bit as much as she did, Brice was glad to comply. Over cups of cappuccino, he told Karen about being a health nut as a teenager, then an exercise nut as he'd matured. Over a split order of English trifle, he told her of running six miles a day, of entering 10K races, of finding himself that much more energetic after his morning runs. Over refills of the coffee, he told her that she was built for the sport and that she'd enjoy it. And when she was sitting back, utterly replete and feeling like a stuffed pig, he outlined a sample program for getting her started.

She grinned broadly at that, and when Brice grew suddenly serious, when his eyes darkened and focused for a prolonged moment on her mouth, she acknowledged something about their dinner. It had been a delight—peaceful and interesting. It had also been stimulating in ways totally aside from the intellectual. Her body was humming with awareness. She knew that Brice turned her on, but she hadn't expected to feel the heat so strongly in such a public place. He hadn't touched her other than to place a light hand at her back as they'd walked to their table. But she felt him. She felt his height, his strength. She felt the difference between his body and hers. And she felt his eyes, dark gray and alight, sending a message she couldn't ignore.

No man's eyes had lured her like this before. A

flush rose in her cheeks, and she might have made a
fool of herself by starting to stammer about something
totally irrelevant had not Brice regained his own control first and said, ''Shall we go?''

She nodded. He rose, came to her chair and drew
it out as she stood, then took her hand in his and led
her to the door.

For as short and quiet as the drive home was, the
atmosphere in the car was charged. Karen didn't dare
look at Brice lest her eyes reveal her desire. He kept
his gaze rigidly on the road.

Not a word was spoken until they were back in the
house, and then good manners overrode her fears.
''Thank you,'' she said, looking up at him. ''That was
delightful.''

Hanging his coat in the closet, he turned to take
hers, but one look at her brought back his need in a
rush. Only now it was magnified. He hadn't remembered ever enjoying an evening as much. Karen was
lovely to look at, lovely to be with. She was bright
and even-tempered, personable and responsive. And
she'd had eyes only for him. In the midst of a full
restaurant, she'd made him feel like the only man
there. That was the corker. He needed her like a flame
needed fuel.

Before he could deny himself, he lowered his head
and captured her mouth. He kissed her softly, then
with greater force when the answering movement of
her mouth demanded it. But just before he reached
that next step of crushing her body to his, he pulled
back.

"No," he said roughly, to himself as much as to her. "I didn't take you to dinner for this." He snatched her coat from her boneless hands and said in a voice reminiscent of his earliest commands, "Go to bed, Karen."

For a minute she didn't move. She had an intense need to hold him, to feel him, to be held and felt. The fact that she'd never been a toucher was irrelevant. Her empty palms ached to be filled.

But that wasn't all that ached to be filled, and when Karen realized what the hollowness deep down in her belly was, she found the strength to move. Too much had happened too soon. She needed space to think. With a shaky breath and on legs that were little better, she turned and climbed the stairs to bed.

9

Karen spent a good deal of time lying awake in bed that night wondering what would have happened had not Brice ended their kiss when he had. The more she wondered, the more frustrated she grew until sheer tiredness conquered even that. She slept late the next morning. When she awoke, she busied herself with work in an effort to escape the dilemma.

To some extent she succeeded. When she was doing reading assignments or talking with Meg, she wasn't as apt to think of needing Brice. She was apprehensive about being with him that evening, but her fears proved groundless. He said nothing about what had happened the night before, instead engaging her in discussions on various topics that seemed to crop up, one after the other, in easy succession. He was much like his grandmother in that sense, Karen discovered. He was curious. He enjoyed broadening his mind. Since she was the same, the conversation never lagged. And by the time she went to bed, leaving him before the living room fire, she was tired enough not to think about sex.

Friday she worked, then visited Rowena. Friday night Brice took her to see a play that was being staged at the university. Neither of them liked the production, but over sundaes at a local ice-cream shop afterward, they had a good time criticizing playwright and cast.

Saturday morning, telling her that he had to do research, Brice took her to McDonald's for breakfast.

"What kind of research is this?" she asked in bemusement after he'd plopped an Egg McMuffin in front of her.

"I have to keep up on these things for the sake of my kids."

"I think you're just lazy," she teased. "Meg's off for the weekend. It was either this or do it yourself."

"No way. There are restaurants that serve fancier breakfasts. We had a choice." He paused and said more quietly, "I had a choice." He paused again, his eyes deep and questing. "Would you rather I'd made a different one?"

"No way," she echoed him and meant it. Breakfast at McDonald's was a fun thing to do. She hadn't had the luxury of doing many things just for fun in her life. She was enjoying herself. "But I have to get home to work after this."

"You do not."

"Sure, I do. I didn't make it to any classes this week, so I want to get ahead in the syllabus. Next week I'll have to borrow the class notes I missed and copy them. That could take a lot of time on top of regular assignments."

"You're not actually planning to do them by hand, are you?" he asked in a critical tone.

She tipped up her chin. "Do you have a better idea?"

"Xerox them."

"Uh-huh. Thirty-plus pages, plus a dozen in handouts for each of four classes, at ten cents a shot—"

"Use my machine."

She took a quick breath. "You have one?"

He nodded.

Sitting back, Karen mused at how easy he was making her life. His machine could save her hours of work. "On one condition."

"You can't pay me."

"Then let me cook dinner tonight."

He shook his head.

"Why not?" she asked.

"Because I want us to go to an inn that I've been hearing about lately."

Karen studied his eyes. In the shadow of the yellow arches, they were varying shades of gray. She saw an odd mixture of determination and unsureness in their depths, plus something else. She sensed that he was discovering the same hunger for human companionship that she was. Loners they might have been, but something happened when they got together. Brice could have gone to McDonald's a million other times before. But who wanted to go to McDonald's alone?

So they went to the inn for dinner that night, but that was after a full day of running errands. Brice decided that the freezer was low, so they went to the supermarket. Then they went antiquing, searching for an early-American bench for Brice's front porch.

Then they went to the camera store to buy film and darkroom supplies, which sparked an entirely new discussion when Karen learned why a camera had been lying around in the den.

She was fascinated by his being a photographer, albeit a closet one. No one ever saw his pictures. But she wanted to, and she wore him down enough so that after a late lunch at a local mall, he gave in. When they returned to the house, he dropped a box in her lap and left her to examine its contents while he busied himself elsewhere.

Karen was in awe. Working entirely in black and white, he'd photographed houses, churches, trees, horses, fences—all from unusual angles and with the eye for light that Karen read praised so often in her books. He'd photographed places he'd visited— Alaska, New Zealand, the Aran Isles, Madagascar. But mostly, he'd photographed his kids. Apparently there was an outdoor waiting room, a play area in the yard during spring, summer and fall. There he'd taken some of the most touching pictures she'd ever seen.

When she said so, he got defensive. "I wasn't looking for praise."

"I know, but I'm offering it anyway."

"Well, don't. It's a hobby. That's all."

"But you're good at it."

"So?"

"So maybe you'll teach me. I'm an art history major, I've been reading about light and shadow and shape and form for years, but I can't draw. Maybe I can do this."

Apparently she'd said the right thing, because Brice warmed back up, which was not to say that he had her in the darkroom the next day. He had other things in mind—such as taking her to a chamber music concert Sunday afternoon, then a movie that night.

When Monday arrived, she was no more ahead on her work than she'd been when she'd set it aside on Friday. Oddly, that didn't bother her as it once might have. She'd had a wonderful weekend. She was feeling stronger and more rested.

And she was in love.

That was why she never quite got into the article on the Newars of the Kathmandu Valley when she visited Rowena on Tuesday. There were more urgent things she wanted to discuss.

With little preamble, she said in a soft voice, "Tell me about Brice."

Rowena didn't even blink in surprise. "He's my grandson. He's a doctor. He's thirty-nine and s-s-single."

"What was he like as a little boy?"

"Ask him."

"He doesn't like to talk about himself. He'll beat around the bush or change the subject."

"W-w-why do you think that is?"

"Because he's hiding something," Karen said. While she wasn't ready to admit to Rowena that she was in love with the man, she had nothing to lose by being honest about her thoughts and observations. "Something happened earlier today. John Parker, Brice's friend, drove me back to Syracuse for two classes. I got back in time for a late lunch, but Meg was out and I didn't feel like eating alone. So I went looking for Brice. He was with a patient.''

''You knew he would be,'' Rowena remarked.

''Yes. I guess...I guess I just wanted to tell him I was back.'' She'd wanted to see him, it was as simple as that, but when she'd arrived at the office, she hadn't had time for regrets. ''He was in one of the examining rooms, but the door was open. There was Brice, a little girl who couldn't have been more than three and her mother. Brice was holding the child, talking to her.''

She paused for a minute, recalling the scene. It had touched her deeply. ''He was wonderful—his voice, expression, arms all gentle. I mean, he wasn't gooing and gaaing. He wasn't playing with the child, but he was so...*sweet* with her. Then her mother asked a question and the softness disappeared. His entire manner changed. He became shuttered.'' She took a breath. ''He doesn't relate well with adults. I've noticed it a lot.''

''He relates with you.''

''Now, but only because he knows me. He didn't at first. And he bluntly acknowledges that he dislikes adults. There has to be a reason. He relates to the wounded, but it's like he has a chip on his shoulder when it comes to the strong ones.''

Rowena sat quietly for a minute. ''You are very p-p-perceptive.''

But not perceptive enough, Karen rued. ''Why does he do it?''

"Because he *is* the wounded."

"He's as hale and hardy as you and I would ever want to be!"

"He wasn't always."

That hadn't occurred to Karen. "He was sick as a child?"

Rowena made a tiny, almost imperceptible movement of her head that, magnified, would have been a nod.

"What did he have?"

"Nothing d-d-deadly. Obviously. He had asthma and...j-j-juvenile rheumatoid arthritis."

"My God."

"All outgrown. He's fine now."

"But that he should have had one of those, let alone both..." Her heart ached for the sickly child he'd been.

"Other children weren't always k-k-kind to him. He was small for his age. And s-s-spindly. He couldn't play sports. They made fun of him. S-s-so he turned his back on them."

Karen was beginning to understand. "He read and studied. He did well in school, went to college, then medical school. Somewhere along the line he got physically stronger and larger."

"His senior year in h-h-high school. He was a handsome boy, then. But not happy. He wanted r-r-revenge."

"Did he get it?" Karen asked warily.

"Mmm."

"How?"

"He stole pretty girls from other boys, then dropped them. He wrote s-s-scathing editorials in the school newspaper. He ran away w-w-with achievement awards others wanted."

"But if he got his revenge, why hasn't he put all that behind him?"

"It's...p-p-part of his personality. Has been since he was three. All the formative years. He is cynical."

Karen began to see it. The chip had taken root on his shoulder when he was too young to understand, and by the time he was old enough, he just didn't care. He had his life, his career. He made sure that he wasn't beholden to anyone.

"Didn't his parents see what was happening?" Karen asked. It seemed there should be someone to blame. "Didn't they get him into counseling?"

"They married late. His father—m-m-my son—was in business. His mother was a social b-b-butterfly. They were busy. They saw what they wanted to see."

"Brice told me about the summers and vacations he spent with you."

"I did what I could. It wasn't enough."

Gazing off toward the window, Karen considered that. Brice did have a productive life. He had far more than many people dreamed of having. But his personal life was stunted.

She knew that he enjoyed himself with her, that he'd enjoyed all the things they'd done together. "I could help him," she murmured. "I know I could."

"Yes," Rowena said.

Karen looked at her. "But I can't help if he won't let me, and I won't help if I'm going to end up hurt. I want a little happiness out of this, too." She glanced away. "If only we'd met under other circumstances."

"You didn't."

"I know."

"Trust him, Karen."

"I want to."

"Y-y-you can."

Karen eyed her sadly then. "Can you guarantee that he won't look at me once or twice a week and remember what I did to you?"

"You weren't at fault," the old woman said with the conviction that only she and Karen could share.

"But does he believe that?"

"Ask him."

"I can't. I can't."

"Why not?"

Why not? Karen conjured up images of the Brice she'd first seen, the man whose hateful stare had haunted her during her trial. She heard echoes of harshness, of sarcasm and pointedness in his voice—echoes from those early days at his house. Why couldn't she ask him whether, deep down inside, he still held a grudge?

"Because," she murmured despairingly, "because I'm afraid I won't like his answer."

It was a matter of trust, she decided. That was what it boiled down to. Karen trusted Brice with her care. She trusted that he'd never physically do her harm.

She trusted that he had the ability to make her happy.
But she didn't know whether he would *choose* to do
so, and that was where her trust lagged.

Her discussion with Rowena had helped. Knowing
what Brice had been through as a child enabled her
to better understand what made him the man he was.
It also made her see how far he'd come with her. She
was, theoretically, no longer one of the wounded, still
he wanted her with him. He spent all his free time
with her. And he desired her.

Oh yes, he desired her. He hadn't kissed her in
days, but he wanted to. She could tell by the way his
eyes would go dark when he looked at her—not dark,
as in angry, but dark, as in hungry and hot. Whenever
it happened, he looked quickly away, but not quickly
enough to spare her the frustration. Because, whether
he was looking at her or not, whether she was looking
at him or not, she was never far from a state of arousal
where Brice was concerned.

She had studied him long and hard. She had stolen
glances while they'd been walking down streets,
while they'd been waiting in lines, while they'd been
moving around each other in the house. She had, often and with hidden pleasure, imagined every inch of
him naked. She no longer needed to look. He was
engraved on her mind. She wanted him.

That knowledge was never far from her during that
second week at his house. Each morning she returned
to Syracuse, either for classes or to work in the li-
brary. Each afternoon, except for the two when she

visited Rowena, she studied. And her evenings were spent with Brice.

She was in love. She was in need, and though the fear of making a one-sided commitment remained, the ache grew deeper and deeper. It was no wonder, then, that when Brice suggested they bring in pizza for an early dinner on Friday and spend the evening in the darkroom, Karen had serious doubts about the plan. A darkroom was asking for trouble; temptation would be magnified in such a close environment, and she wasn't sure she could handle it. But he seemed so eager, in his own understated way, that she couldn't refuse.

The darkroom was in the basement of the house and fortunately, wasn't as small as Karen had feared it would be. Nor was it as dark. At the start, when Brice was mixing chemicals, filling trays, organizing the negatives he wanted to print and gathering miscellaneous small tools, bare bulbs lit the room. When those bulbs went off, her eyes easily adjusted to the dim glow cast by the two red safelights that were strung above the long worktable.

Brice wasn't a talkative teacher, clearly more of the show than tell school. Without a word, he put the first negative in the carrier, slipped it into the enlarger, adjusted the image to his satisfaction, put photographic paper in the easel and made a test exposure. Still without a word, he slipped the paper into the developer solution and began to rock the tray.

Though Karen had never been in a darkroom before, she was aware of what was going to happen, so she wasn't totally surprised when a form began to appear on the paper. What surprised her was the incredible beauty of the image.

Catching her breath as Brice transferred the paper into the stop bath, she stared at it through its minutes-long immersion in the fixer. The child she saw was very young, very small, very dirty and, if its ragged clothes were any indication, very poor.

"A patient?" she asked in a whisper.

Hooking a forefinger under the corner of the tray, Brice rocked it just lightly enough to ensure that the solution worked evenly over the surface of the print. "Former patient. His family left the area three months ago looking to live where they wouldn't have to worry about heat. Both parents were unskilled and unemployed. It didn't matter much where they went."

Karen said nothing more, because the photograph said it all. Brice had captured despair in a child who was probably too young to understand what it meant.

When the print was fixed, he turned on a white light and studied it. "Needs more contrast, I think." He pointed to a corner of the print that was lighter than the rest. "And a little more time here." He dropped the print in a tub of clear water, turned off the light and repeated the printing procedure, making the changes he wanted. When that print had been fixed and examined, he decided that he wanted it cropped more tightly. So, after adjusting the height of the enlarger head, he made a third print. When all three lay in the holding tub, he took a different negative and made a trial print.

This one was a world away from the first. It was the typical small-child-with-cone-in-hand-and-ice-cream-on-face shot, but there was nothing typical about the child—as devilish-looking a one as Karen had ever seen—or the technical perfection of the photograph.

On the heels of that came a silhouette of three children of different heights peering through a chain-link playground fence, then one of a pair of identical twin toddlers studying each other through the rungs of a ladder.

By this time, Brice had Karen doing the work. Quietly and succinctly, he explained the purpose of each step and advised her about exposure and development times. When the small cordless phone that he kept in the corner of the room rang, she was perfectly capable of carrying on for the few minutes until he returned.

"Problem?" she asked. She dropped the last print she'd done into clear water and looked up at him. He didn't look pleased.

"Yeah. I'm going to have to run over to the hospital in a few minutes."

"What's wrong?"

"Car accident. One of my patients—a boy—was tossed around a little."

Karen felt her pulse beating faster. "How old?"

"Five."

"Go," she urged.

"Not yet. He'll be in X-ray a while longer, and the orthopedic specialist will take him from there. The parents called me mainly for reassurance that they'd done everything they should have.''

''Was one of them driving?''

''No. The boy was in the car with his grandmother. He was the only one injured—has a broken arm, possibly some ribs. He'll be fine, but they'll want to keep him at the hospital overnight, and his mother says he's terrified. If I'm there when they finally get him into a room, I may be able to help settle him down.''

''I think that's nice,'' Karen said with an admiring smile.

Brice frowned and said gruffly, ''I don't. I really wanted to work longer here. Come on. Let's see what we can get done in another twenty or thirty minutes. Then I'll go.''

''Are you sure you wouldn't rather leave now? I'll be—''

''I'm not leaving you alone with my negatives.''

She studied his face through the dim red light. He looked serious. ''I won't steal them.''

''You might scratch them. One scratch, and the negative's no good.''

''Have I scratched one yet?''

''You've only *handled* one.''

''And did I scratch it?'' she asked indignantly. She didn't like being talked down to, particularly when she'd done nothing to warrant it.

''No.''

''So I'm not a lost cause. And now that you've warned me, I can be careful.''

''I warned you at the very start to be careful.''

"About fingerprints. Not scratches."

"Jeez, you don't give up, do you?"

"Do you?"

Silence stretched between them for what seemed an eternity before Karen finally turned back to the enlarger, very carefully removed the negative, very carefully returned it to its sleeve and said, "What's next?"

Brice reached for another sleeve, but his thoughts were on what he'd just said. *Jeez, you don't give up, do you?* She didn't, and that was one of the things that drew him to her again and again. She wasn't intimidated. She wasn't driven away when he was raunchy. For all her fragile looks, she was a strong woman.

Changing his mind about what print to make, he replaced the strip of negatives he'd just taken with another. Karen wasn't prepared to see her own face appear on the enlarger easel.

"When did you take this?" she cried.

He leaned in over her shoulder. "At the mall."

"I thought you were photographing the fountain."

"I was. You got in the way."

Karen studied the projection. "I look awful."

"You look like you're enjoying yourself."

"I look like a fat cat."

"Not fat."

"Then content. And lazy."

"You look very relaxed."

With his warmth close behind her and the image on the easel bringing back lovely memories, she felt more tranquil than she had moments before. "I was listening to the fountain. It reminded me of a bubbling brook, and I was thinking how nice it would be to be out in the woods by the water's edge and…just sit. It was nice sitting right there in the middle of a mall. Just sitting. Not working. Not thinking about working. Not running around or thinking about running around. Just sitting." She felt his body touch hers and relaxed against it. It felt so right. "A tiny voice in the back of my mind kept telling me that I should have been feeling guilty, but I wasn't."

"In hindsight, do you?"

"This is the wrong time to ask. Ask when I'm opening my books to do all the work I should have done last week."

He slipped his arms around her waist. "I'm asking you now."

Closing her eyes, she said, "No. I don't feel guilty now." She didn't think she could possibly feel anything but good just then.

"Do you feel guilty about staying at my house?"

"Sometimes."

"Why?"

"I'm not a freeloader."

"But do you enjoy staying here?"

She hesitated, distracted by the feel of his breath against her cheek. She moved her head the tiniest bit to feel the roughness of his jaw on her skin. "Yes," she breathed. "I enjoy staying here." When his mouth dropped to her neck, she tipped her head to give him better access. "I do enjoy it here," she whispered. "I shouldn't. It's habit-forming. And I'll have to leave soon." Unable to resist, she covered his hands with hers, then followed their movement when his fingers began a gentle massage of her tummy. They left wonderful circles of heat. She sighed in pleasure.

Buoyed by that tiny sound, Brice dragged his mouth back and forth against her neck. He loved the smell of her, loved the softness of her skin. He'd tried to stay away, but he needed to touch her now. "You can stay here."

She made a small, breathless sound. "Not forever. My life is back in Syracuse."

One of his hands moved higher, steadily massaging until it brushed the undersides of her breasts. "It doesn't have to be."

"Sure, it does," she said, but her voice was strained. Her breasts were waiting, needing, swelling. "My apartment is there, my jobs, my classes."

"You've been handling everything fine from here."

"No…" She caught in a breath when he covered her breast, then whispered his name in such a way that other words weren't necessary.

"It's okay," he said softly. "Just relax."

Her voice came out several notes higher. "You shouldn't be doing this. You have to leave."

"Shhhh." He moved his hand slowly over her full-ness. The fleece of her pullover sweat suit top was a soft conduit for the sensual flame of his touch.

"Brice…"

His other hand rose to mirror the motion of its mate, fingers circling, palms pressing, kneading her to awareness. His voice was as husky as her insides were beginning to feel when he said, "I like having you here."

She turned her head against his chest. "But I can't stay forever."

"You promised me until vacation was done."

"I know."

"There's nothing for you back in Syracuse."

"Not right now."

She gasped. He had slipped his hands under her sweatshirt and was touching her breasts more intimately.

"Easy...easy," he whispered when she seemed to have trouble catching her breath. Her hands had fallen and were curved tightly around the backs of his thighs.

He took her earlobe into his mouth and sucked on it to the rhythm of his thumbs. "I like touching you."

"You have to leave," she said, aching at the thought.

"Not yet." He nipped at her ear, then while she was recovering from that, released the front catch of her bra and took her turgid flesh in his hands.

She moaned.

But his fingers were magic, and the flow of his deep voice gentled her. "Ahhh, Karen, so soft...like silk...womanly warm." With deliberate care, he rolled the pad of his thumbs over her nipples. Already engorged, they grew painfully tight.

But that sweet pain wasn't only in her breasts. It was deep down in her belly, and it was spreading. Her breath came more shallowly, catching every so often in her throat. Somewhere in the back of her mind, she knew Brice had to stop, though for the life of her she couldn't hasten the moment. What he was doing to her felt too good. Besides, the fact that he had to leave was the safety valve she needed. Nothing of true consequence could possibly happen.

Then one of his hands left a breast and slid downward, and she stiffened. "Brice?" she cried in a tremulous voice. "What are you doing, Brice?"

His hand reached its goal. She made a convulsive move to escape it, but that only drove her into the masculine heat raging behind.

"Shhhh," he murmured hoarsely. "I want to give you pleasure...."

She gripped his thighs tightly and gasped, "You are." Then she turned her cheek sharply to his chest and bit her lip when small whimpers threatened to reveal just how pleased she was.

His hands were relentless. While one continued to taunt her nipple, the other slid under the band of her sweatpants, breached the barrier of her panties and found her darkest, most moist heart.

Hit by a sudden stroke of fire, she did cry out then. She begged him to stop, but he didn't listen, and there was nothing her traitorous body would do to free her from the onslaught. His fingers were parting her, caressing her, delving ever deeper into her hidden warmth. She wanted to fight—it was too much, too strong—but the wave of sensation was even stronger, and before she'd been able to whimper more than a few cries of protest, she was sucking in her breath, closing her fists on the corduroy of his jeans and arching her back into a powerful release.

Her body was still trembling and her breathing ragged when she covered her face with her hands and made soft, mortified sounds.

"Don't," Brice commanded in a low and shaky voice.

"I'm sorry," came her muffled cry. "That shouldn't have happened."

"Don't say that," he replied even more gruffly.

"I'm embarrassed."

"Because you're a woman who feels passion to the fullest?" He turned her to face him with perhaps more force than was necessary, but he wasn't going to let her besmirch the pleasure she'd felt. Taking her face in his hands, he tipped it up. His voice was deep and rough. "That happened because it should have. It's been coming for days."

She tried to shake her head, but he allowed little movement. Still she could talk. "No. What's been coming for days is our making love. But what happened just now was one-sided. I should have been able to stop."

"I didn't let you."

"Then it's your fault, too."

"My fault for *what*? What's so bad about what happened?"

"You got nothing out of it!"

That caught him for a minute. "Are you serious?"

She tried to break away, but he simply enfolded her in his arms and held her close.

"See?" she said. "You're not satisfied. I can feel you…feel you there…."

She was looking so pink-cheeked, even under the safe lights, that Brice had a sudden urge to laugh. "I'm still hard," he admitted. "I've been hard for the better part of a week. And if it weren't for the fact that I'm expected at the hospital, I'd carry you upstairs and make love to you well." He set her back. "We will make love, Karen. At least, we will if you stay here another night. So maybe it's just as well that I have to leave now. You'll have some time to think about whether you want what I do." He took a step away.

"You're going?" she asked dumbly. She was still shaky. And he was still aroused.

"Yes."

"You can't leave just…just like that."

"Why not?"

Her gaze fell to his fly.

"I'll live," he said.

"But what about—" She turned and looked at the enlarger head, still projecting a picture of her face.

"Leave it. I'll clean up when I get back."

With that said—and not trusting himself to say anything more—he was gone.

10

Karen barely slept that night. She was lying in bed when Brice returned from the hospital at one o'clock in the morning. By two, he still hadn't come to her, and by three she realized that he didn't plan to.

She was disappointed, frustrated and hurt.

By the time dawn rolled around, she was heartsick. Hoping that a glass of warm milk might soothe her, she crept softly through the still-dark halls to the kitchen. On its threshold, she stopped, frozen in place by the sight before her.

Brice was standing with his back to her. His arms were straight, hands flat on the tiled countertop. His head was bowed. But it wasn't his pose that held her breathless. It was the fact that he'd carelessly kicked his running shoes aside, just as carelessly scattered his wool hat and mittens, running suit and turtleneck jersey on the table and chairs—which left him wearing nothing but a thin pair of nylon running shorts and a sheen of sweat.

Her pulse began to race. She'd imagined so often how he'd look beneath his clothes, but her imaginings paled before the real thing. He was all man. His shoulders were made broad by twists of muscle that tapered gently down his arms and torso. She'd known to expect that tapering, but she hadn't expected such symmetry, muscles flanking his spine from shoulder to hip. Nor had she expected such smooth skin. Or such tight buttocks. Or such long, well-formed legs.

She'd found him attractive before, but she'd never experienced such a sudden flood of desire. And then, slowly, he turned and she was lost. His chest was sculpted, an artistic creation of bone, muscle and flesh. He wasn't hairy; only a thin sprinkling of dark hair dotted his upper chest, condensing into an even thinner line that arrowed downward. His legs were more hairy, but his legs weren't what drew Karen's attention. It was his sex, blatantly heavy as it was cradled by the soft nylon fabric.

Aware that everything inside her was swelling and moist, she dragged her eyes up. His were dark and vulnerable, sensual and questioning. In answer, knowing that the love she felt had no more appropriate outlet than this, she silently crossed the floor to stand before him. Lifting one trembling hand, she touched his skin.

It was hot and damp and vibrant. She slid her hand over it, opening her palm on the more textured spots, splaying her fingers to better delineate virile swells of muscle. Her touch was light, feathery. His sweat was a lubricant, easing the flow of her hand, and when her skin stuttered against his, it was in pure awe.

From one shoulder to the other and down, she explored him in wonder. Touching both hands to his upper arms, she whispered an open trail over corded lines to his wrists, then rose on an upward route from his waist.

His nipples were small, tight dots. She moved her thumbs over them simply to know their feel. When Brice inhaled suddenly, she looked up.

His hair was a riot of darkness, rendered that way by his wool cap and sweat. His face was rough with a day's growth of beard. His lips were tense with need. His nostrils flared slightly with each breath. And his eyes burned for her.

She touched his cheek. She touched his hair, allowing only her fingertips burial in the vibrant thatch. She touched his lips with her thumb. She touched his jaw, then his ear with the back of her hand. Then she touched him as she desperately wanted to, lip to lip.

The kiss was slow, tentative and exploratory at first, more sure as Brice joined in, then more thorough. It was the intermingling of breath, the glide of one tongue against another, the scrape of teeth against lips and chin. It was open-mouthed and erotic, and if there had been any doubt about a mutual desire, this kiss put it to rest.

Hands framing her face, Brice paused. He would never get enough of looking at her when she was hot with needing him. And she was. He could feel, hear, taste her arousal as clearly as he could see it.

That minute's exchanged glance was all they needed. Their open mouths met again, but now their hands were busy. Hers lowered his shorts to free his sex, while his drew up her nightshirt. Then, while their tongues delved deeply into each other's mouths, Brice lifted her and thrust into her warmth.

Karen cried out at the sudden fullness, but a rare beauty overpowered the slight pain she felt. Arms coiled around his neck, she panted, whispered fragmented words of love.

Brice squeezed his eyes shut. He held himself still inside her partly to let her adjust to his size, partly to control his own blazing need for release. She was a hot, tight glove around him; after years of abstinence, she was nearly a virgin. But he tried not to think of that, because it set his blood to rushing even harder.

Forehead to forehead they stood, their breathing fast and ragged. Brice turned until she was braced against the counter, then with trembling hands stroked the length of her legs as they wound around his hips. When he felt her insides flex, he took her mouth again and began to move his hips. What followed then was a passion that snowballed with such speed that neither of them quite knew what had seized them until it was over.

It was a while before their gasps faded into the dawn air, a while after that before either of them could move. Brice leaned against Karen, who leaned against the counter. His head was bowed low over her shoulder, hair damp, skin damp, arms limp, hands locked behind her. Her own circled his neck as she buried her face in his shoulder. Her hair hung wild and loose. Her legs clung to him with stubborn strength.

She made a small sound of protest when he separated himself from her. "Just for a minute," he whispered. Kicking his shorts aside, he swept her into his arms and carried her up the stairs to his bedroom. There, he drew off her nightshirt and laid her on the bed, then proceeded to love her with the kind of gentle finesse that neither of them had been able to abide earlier. Not until he'd touched and tasted every inch of her body did he enter her, and then he led her to a peak of pleasure that left her dazed.

That was why she wasn't sure she heard right when he said he loved her.

She eyed him blankly. "You what?"

"Love you."

Snaking an arm across his chest, she pressed her face to his damp skin. Then she inched up until she could reach his mouth, and kissed him softly. One part of her wanted to jump for joy; the other part was frightened. "Do you?"

"Yes."

"Why?"

"What do you mean, 'Why'?"

"What do you find to love in me?"

Brice tucked in his chin and looked down at her. He couldn't believe what she was asking, but she seemed entirely serious. "I think you're bright and interesting. You're a hard worker. You're curious and compassionate."

"You're saying that you respect me."

"Isn't respect the basis of love?"

"You can respect a woman without being in love with her."

He was silent.

"So what is it?" she prodded softly. "What do you feel, deep down inside?"

"I feel like I want you here with me forever," he said in a voice that was rough but not begrudging. "I've never felt that way before."

"You must have when you got married."

"No. I was thinking that I should be married, and I was envisioning the immediate future. That's all. I wasn't thinking forever."

She searched his eyes. "Are you now?"

Very slowly he nodded.

Karen tightened her arms around him in an attempt to get even closer to him than she already was. It was an impossibility, but still she tried because the closer she was, the more he filled her senses, and the more he did that, the less she thought about the one thing that could ruin it all.

After a minute, her arms began to tremble. After another minute, her shoulders did, too. That was when Brice got worried.

"Karen?"

She didn't answer.

"Karen?" Sliding his hands under her arms, he raised her. The sight of tears in her eyes brought a lump of fear to his chest. Easing her down to the bed, he lifted himself over her and said in a voice that shook, "What's wrong?"

She didn't answer at first, simply looked up into his face. His expression was as tender as any she'd ever seen there, which choked her up all the more.

Only after several sniffles and a swallow did she manage to say, "I love you, too." Then she threw her arms around his neck and silently bid him hold her for as long as he could…or would.

Brice would have been the happiest man alive if he hadn't been as attuned to the fine points of emotions. Just because he was a loner didn't mean he didn't see things. Just because he chose not to play social games didn't mean he didn't understand why others did. His specialty demanded a certain insight into the nonphysical side of life. He had that insight, to some extent.

He believed that Karen loved him. He believed that she wanted the same forever he did. But something bothered her, and he didn't know what it was.

Not once were they apart on Saturday. Nor were they sleepy, though neither had slept the night before. Running on adrenaline, they spent most of the morning making love, most of the afternoon driving to the western part of the state, most of the evening making love in the small room they'd taken for the night in a quaint bed-and-breakfast place.

Karen smiled, and smiled often, and Brice appreciated that for the victory it was. But she didn't smile as broadly as he wanted. She didn't smile with the kind of carefree indulgence that she deserved.

So he began to attack her possible worries one by one.

He wondered if she thought he'd want her to quit school. While they were driving back to Ithaca on

Sunday afternoon, he said in no uncertain terms that he thought she should finish, that he was sure she could transfer to Cornell at the end of the year if she wanted to, and, if not, she could continue to commute to Syracuse.

He wondered if she thought he'd want her to quit her jobs. He did, so he broached that one more gently. They were on their way home from visiting Rowena on Sunday evening—their first joint visit, noted well by Rowena, whose eyes were filled with pleasure and speculation—when he asked what Karen thought about work.

"That depends," she said quietly. Her eyes were on the road. "I want to do something with my degree once I get it, but I want to have kids. I'm not sure I can do both and do either well."

Unprepared for that particular answer, Brice took a minute to catch his breath. He would have hugged her had it not been for the BMW's bucket seats. As second best, he took her hand and held it tightly in his. "If anyone can, it's you," he said and cleared his throat. "But that's something we have time to discuss. I was thinking more about now. You don't have to work. You won't need the money—" he rushed on "—but if you want to work, I'll understand. The only problem is that your hours at the Pepper Mill aren't great. If you stay on there, we won't have much time to spend together, so I was thinking that you could keep on with McGuire if you want—"

"I'd rather be here," she said softly.

He took his eyes from the road long enough to shoot her a glance. "You would?"

"Do you mind?"

"Hell, no!"

So that issue was settled, and by the time Monday rolled around, Karen was studying for midterms. Rather than broaching any others, he concentrated on pampering her and doing all he could to be supportive while she studied.

By the end of the week, though, when her exams were done, he faced it again. She was clearly relieved and looking forward to vacation. But still she held back. He felt it in the way she occasionally touched his arm, then pulled away. He heard it in the catch at the end of a laugh. He saw it in a flicker of worry that passed through her eyes so quickly that he probably would have missed it if he didn't care so much. But he did care. He cared more than he'd ever have thought possible. He wanted Karen to be happy. He was determined to make her happy. It was quickly becoming an obsession.

Failing to pinpoint the source of her worry, he decided that he had to be more blunt—which was a laugh, he mused, since he was notorious for his bluntness. But he was different with Karen. Less abrasive…less defensive…less blunt. She hadn't wanted to live in a war zone, so he'd declared peace. Now, though, a little prodding was in order.

So, Friday night, after he'd wined her and dined her to celebrate the start of her vacation, after he'd made love to her before the living room fire—with a tenderness he hadn't thought himself capable of—he turned on his side and faced her.

"Something's bothering you," he said quietly. "What is it?"

"Nothing's bothering me," she answered with a smile—that smile that was bright enough to fool anyone but him.

"Something is."

She shook her head and reached up to trace the line of his mouth. Then, grabbing his ear, she pulled him close for a kiss, and when the kiss was done, she asked whether he liked apple pancakes, which she wanted to make for breakfast. When he said that he loved them, but only with real maple syrup, that started a discussion about the sugaring season, which effectively changed the subject.

Brice let it go. But again on Sunday, when he caught her staring pensively out the window, he asked what was bothering her. Again she denied that anything was.

On Monday night, when she couldn't concentrate on the book she was reading, he repeated the question. She smiled, said she was a little tired and fell asleep soon after with her head in his lap.

On Wednesday, he asked again, this time when she was unable to make a decision on what kind of engagement ring she wanted. She simply wound her arm tightly through his, pressed her cheek to his shoulder and begged for a little more time.

On Thursday, he didn't ask, but he spent much of the evening watching her pretend involvement in a movie. He felt stymied. He was beginning to imagine that, deep down inside, she didn't want to get married. When he couldn't come up with any viable reasons why that should be so, he began to come up with bizarre ones.

By Friday, he was feeling insecure. Karen meant the world to him. In the short time they'd been together, she'd changed his life. She'd given it vibrancy and flux. She'd made it exciting. When he was with her, he felt complete, satisfied, richer than he had. He'd stopped fighting ghosts. He was more pleasantly disposed toward the rest of mankind because of the happiness she brought him.

The thought that for some mysterious reason he might lose her unsettled him, and when he was unsettled, he withdrew into himself and frowned a lot. That was precisely how he was when, finishing up early with his patients on Friday afternoon, he went with Karen to visit Rowena.

Karen wasn't oblivious to his mood. "Bad day?" she asked as he drove stony-faced toward the home.

"It was okay."

"Any problem cases?"

"Nope."

She was quiet then, but two minutes later he was still frowning. So she said, "Do you still want to drive to Vermont tomorrow?"

"Yes."

"You're sure there's snow?"

"There's snow on Killington Peak until the Fourth of July."

"Won't I slow you down?" She'd never skied before, but he had insisted that she try it.

"You won't slow me down," he said, sounding as though he meant it—and as though her slowing him down was the last of his concerns. She wondered what the first of them was.

So, when they'd turned into the drive of the nursing home, she abandoned beating around the bush and asked, "Is something wrong?"

"Nope."

"You don't look thrilled to be here."

"I'm not. I'd rather be visiting my grandmother anywhere but here."

Karen didn't say another word. Wishing she'd left well enough alone, she climbed from the car and accompanied him inside.

Rowena was waiting for them. She was filled with questions, wanting to know how Karen was feeling, what she was doing with her time, whether she was enjoying the rest. She asked Brice about his work, inquired about the progress of a patient he'd mentioned before, expressed pleasure when he told her that the recent article he'd written on psychosomatic illness in children had been accepted for publication.

She asked whether they'd made a decision on the engagement ring, and Karen said no. She asked whether Karen had moved the last of her things from her apartment, and Karen said no. She mentioned that one of the other women in the home had gone out that afternoon to pick out a dress for her granddaughter's wedding, and Karen didn't say a thing.

Rowena fell silent. Karen smiled at her. Brice did the same. They were sharing a large winged chair, Brice on the seat, Karen propped on the arm. Rowena's eyes shifted slowly from one face to the other, then she said as clearly as if she'd never had a stroke, "This is a mistake."

Brice frowned. "What is?"

"You two."

"What do you mean?" Karen asked.

But Rowena's eyes were on Brice. "Y-y-you shouldn't be together. You won't forget what happened."

Karen's heart began to hammer against her ribs. She'd thought that Rowena was all for a union between Brice and her. Confused, she looked at Brice, but he was scowling at his grandmother.

"I think you'd better explain yourself," he said in a controlled voice.

Rowena didn't hesitate. "Karen was driving the car that hit me."

"She wasn't at fault."

"But she w-w-was driving."

"She was tried and found not guilty."

"What do juries know?"

"Rowena..." he warned softly.

But Rowena wasn't to be stopped. "Karen hit me. A j-j-jury found her not guilty. The legal...c-c-case is closed, but you still believe she was at fault. How can you think of s-s-spending the rest of your life with her?"

Brice leaned forward and put his elbows on his

knees. His fists didn't quite hang. "I don't believe she was at fault."

"You did."

"Maybe once. Not now."

Rowena sat and stared silently at him, daring him to defend his switch. He had no problem with that.

"I needed someone to blame for what had happened to you. I couldn't very well vent my anger on the moon that wasn't out that night or the narrowness of the road or that excuse of a bicycle you were riding. Karen was there. She was it. But I've gotten to know her since. There isn't a negligent, a reckless or unkind bone in her body."

Rowena let that declaration settle for a minute before she said, "You're in love. That m-m-makes you blind."

Brice's shoulders were growing more tense by the minute. "I don't think," he said in a low, sharp voice, "that there is any point to this discussion."

Rowena disagreed. "There is. You offered...h-h-her your services when she was s-s-sick because you knew she'd...been...visiting me. But she's fine now. Isn't talk of marriage carrying hospitality too far?"

"I don't believe I'm hearing this," he muttered and glanced at Karen. "What's the matter with her?"

Karen couldn't answer. She was too busy studying Rowena's face, trying to figure things out herself.

The older woman's mouth puckered. "It's a betrayal."

"That's bullshit."

"Don't use that l-l-language with me, Brice Carlin."

He drew himself straight. "I'll use whatever language I want." His features were tight. "And there's no other word that better describes what you're saying. I don't understand you. You were the one who had Karen coming here first. I thought you liked her."

"I'm not the one planning to marry her."

"Damn right you're not," he said, coming to his feet with a slow grace that was downright intimidating. Karen had shifted her stare from Rowena to him, but he barely noticed. He was too intent on setting the record straight. "I'm the one in love with her, I'm the one who'll marry her, I'm the one planning to spend the rest of my life with her, and I won't stand for a repeat of the kind of things you've just said.

"Karen was no more at fault for that accident than you were. I freely admit that I thought it once, but I was wrong, and I refuse to make the same mistake twice. The accident happened. It's over. Done. I won't have Karen feeing guilty, and I won't let you make *me* feel guilty."

"Don't you...c-c-care about me?" Rowena asked with an odd meekness. An odd meekness. It brought Karen's wide eyes back to her face.

Brice's, meanwhile, was ruddy with tension and frustration. "I love you, damn it. You mean more to me than my own parents did. I'd do nearly anything to make you happy. But I won't let you sabotage the one thing that means more to me and more to my future than anything else in the world. If it's sabotage you have in mind, Rowena, you can kiss Karen and me goodbye, because, so help me, I swear—''

Karen caught his arm. ''Don't, Brice,'' she whispered.

He turned on her with eyes full of fury. ''I won't have her saying that we don't belong together.''

''She's not—''

''She is! She's saying that the accident will always be between us, but she's wrong. I haven't thought about the accident in days.''

''Yes, you have,'' Karen argued softly. ''You mentioned it when we were driving over here.''

''I did?''

''You were in a lousy mood, and when I asked about it, you said that you'd rather be visiting Rowena anywhere but here.''

''And I meant it,'' he said, looking confused, ''but that had nothing to do with the accident. It had to do with Rowena's condition—today—right now. I wasn't thinking of how and why she came to be here, and I *certainly* wasn't thinking about the fact that your car hit her. That was an *accident*, Karen.'' He tossed a hand her way. ''It wasn't your fault.'' He gestured toward Rowena. ''It wasn't her fault. It just happened. But it's over. My God, I'm *tired* of thinking about it. Isn't it time we moved on?''

Karen's eyes began to fill with tears.

Immediately, he cupped her face and whispered, ''What is it, babe?''

Clutching his wrists, she closed her eyes for a minute. When she opened them, she dragged his hands to her mouth, kissed both open palms, lowered them to her heart and broke into the kind of smile he'd staked his future on.

He stared at that smile, then widened his gaze to include her whole face. Her eyes were bright with tears, brilliant with love. And the smile remained full and unfettered.

Taking a step closer, he whispered, "That was it. That was it, wasn't it? That was what bothered you. You thought I wouldn't be able to put the accident behind—" His voice broke, and seconds later he'd pulled her from the chair and was holding her close. "I put it behind days ago. When I look at you, I see the woman I love. The accident is something that brought us together," he drew back to meet her gaze, "and I don't care what Rowena says—" His voice broke again, but this time on a note of dawning. He stared at Karen for a minute, then slowly turned toward Rowena.

She was looking as smug as you please.

"Why...you...witch," he said, but fondness underscored each word. "Betrayal—baloney! You made all that up. You did that on purpose—" Eyes widening, his gaze flew back to Karen.

She shook her head. "I didn't know what she was up to until three quarters of the way through her act. I believed her, at first. It hurt," she confessed in a very quiet voice.

His voice, too, grew quiet. Intimate. "Why didn't you ask me? If you were worried about it, you should have asked."

"I didn't want to lose you."

"You wouldn't have."

"But I didn't know that. I've never come so close to having something I wanted so much."

Wrapping his arms around her, he rocked her from side to side. "You have me if you want me."

"I want you." She was on tiptoe with her arms around his neck. Pressing a kiss to his ear, she said, "I also want the pear-shaped diamond, and a small wedding soon and a honeymoon somewhere warm. You choose."

He put a hand in her hair and held her close. "St. Kitts."

"Fine."

"For a week?"

"Great."

"But you're on vacation now. The next time you can get away will be after finals. When's that?"

"May."

"Too hot for St. Kitts. How about London?"

"Is it rainy there then?"

"I think it's rainy there anytime. How about Rio?"

"Not bad."

"Or Yugoslavia—the Dalmation Coast."

When he drew her head back, she smiled up at him. "Interesting."

The smile, ah, the smile. It held promise for such happy tomorrows that he had to force himself to think. "Or Australia. Which will it be?"

"You choose."

"Which will it be?"

"I don't know."

"*Which will it be?*"

"I can't make a decision like this on the spur of the moment."

"Karen…"

"The Dalmation Coast. I want to stay in a huge stone villa overlooking the sea, and I don't want to do anything but lie in the sun, eat, sleep and make love—"

"I think," came Rowena's voice from out of the blue, "that there are s-s-some things my tender ears shouldn't hear. Run along, children. You have p-p-plans to make."

Brice released Karen, who immediately bent over Rowena and gave her a hug. "Thank you," she whispered. Her eyes were moist again, but she couldn't stop smiling.

Rowena's eyes beamed.

Brice leaned in and gave the older woman a peck on the cheek. "You haven't heard the end of this," he warned, and as he straightened he saw the beginnings of a grin on her face. For a minute, he stood and enjoyed it. Then, turning, he took Karen's hand, and they headed home.

Visit us at www.zebrabooks.com

New York Times Bestselling Author

JOAN JOHNSTON

Abigail Dayton has a job to do—trap and relocate a wolf that is threatening local ranches, in an effort to save the species from extinction. Abby knows the breed well: powerful, strong and lean. As rare as it is beautiful. Aggressive when challenged. A predator.

But the description fits both the endangered species she's sworn to protect…and a man she's determined to avoid. Local rancher Luke Granger is a lone wolf, the kind of man who doesn't tame or trust easily. The kind of man who tempts a woman to risk everything.…

Never Tease a Wolf

Available April 2001 wherever paperbacks are sold!

Visit us at www.mirabooks.com

MJJ805

New York Times Bestselling Author

DEBBIE MACOMBER

Buffalo Valley, North Dakota, has become a good place to live—the way it used to be, thirty or forty years ago. People here are feeling confident about the future again.

Stalled lives are moving forward. People are taking risks—on new ventures and on lifelong dreams. And one of those people is local rancher Margaret Clemens, who's finally getting what *she* wants most: marriage to cowboy Matt Eilers. Her friends don't think Matt's such a bargain. But Margaret's aware of Matt's reputation and his flaws. She wants him anyway.

And she wants his baby....

Always DAKOTA

"Popular romance writer Macomber has a gift for evoking the emotions that are at the heart of the genre's popularity."
—*Publishers Weekly*

On sale May 2001 wherever paperbacks are sold!

Visit us at www.mirabooks.com

MIRA®

MDM800

MIRABooks.com

We've got the lowdown on your favorite author!

☆ Read an excerpt of your favorite author's newest book

☆ Check out her bio and read our famous "20 questions" interview

☆ Talk to her in our Discussion Forums

☆ Get the latest information on her touring schedule

☆ Find her current besteller, and even her backlist titles

All this and more available at

www.MiraBooks.com
on Women.com Networks

MEAUT1

If you enjoyed what you just read,
then we've got an offer you can't resist!

Take 2
bestselling novels FREE!
Plus get a FREE surprise gift!

Clip this page and mail it to The Best of the Best™

IN U.S.A.
3010 Walden Ave.
P.O. Box 1867
Buffalo, N.Y. 14240-1867

IN CANADA
P.O. Box 609
Fort Erie, Ontario
L2A 5X3

YES! Please send me 2 free Best of the Best™ novels and my free surprise gift. Then send me 4 brand-new novels every month, which I will receive before they're available in stores. In the U.S.A., bill me at the bargain price of $4.24 plus 25¢ delivery per book and applicable sales tax, if any*. In Canada, bill me at the bargain price of $4.74 plus 25¢ delivery per book and applicable taxes**. That's the complete price and a savings of over 15% off the cover prices—what a great deal! I understand that accepting the 2 free books and gift places me under no obligation ever to buy any books. I can always return a shipment and cancel at any time. Even if I never buy another book from The Best of the Best™, the 2 free books and gift are mine to keep forever. So why not take us up on our invitation. You'll be glad you did!

185 MEN C229
385 MEN C23A

Name	(PLEASE PRINT)	
Address	Apt.#	
City	State/Prov.	Zip/Postal Code

* Terms and prices subject to change without notice. Sales tax applicable in N.Y.
** Canadian residents will be charged applicable provincial taxes and GST.
  All orders subject to approval. Offer limited to one per household.
  ® are registered trademarks of Harlequin Enterprises Limited.

BOB00   ©1998 Harlequin Enterprises Limited

**Secrets, lies, blame and guilt.
Only love and forgiveness can overcome
the mistakes of the past.**

RACHEL LEE

Witt Matlock has carried around a bitter hatred for Hardy
Wingate, the man he holds responsible for the death of his
daughter. And now, twelve years later, the man he blames for
the tragedy is back in his life—and in that of his niece, Joni.

Widow Hannah Matlock has kept the truth about her
daughter Joni's birth hidden for twenty-seven years. Only she
knows that her brother-in-law Witt is Joni's father, and not
her uncle. But with Hardy coming between Witt and Joni,
Hannah knows she must let go of her secret...whatever the
consequences.

A JANUARY CHILL

"A magnificent presence in romantic fiction.
Rachel Lee is an author to treasure forever."
—*Romantic Times*

On sale April 2001 wherever paperbacks are sold!

Visit us at www.mirabooks.com   MRL802

BARBARA
DELINSKY

66579	TWELVE ACROSS	___ $6.99 U.S.	___ $8.50 CAN.
66518	THE STUD	___ $5.99 U.S.	___ $6.99 CAN.
66489	SECRET OF THE STONE	___ $5.99 U.S.	___ $6.99 CAN.
66447	CHANCES ARE	___ $5.50 U.S.	___ $6.50 CAN.
66438	THE REAL THING	___ $5.50 U.S.	___ $6.50 CAN.
66423	BRONZE MYSTIQUE	___ $5.50 U.S.	___ $6.50 CAN.
66287	THE OUTSIDER	___ $5.50 U.S.	___ $6.50 CAN.
66271	HAVING FAITH	___ $5.50 U.S.	___ $6.50 CAN.
66175	THE DREAM COMES TRUE	___ $5.50 U.S.	___ $6.50 CAN.
66161	THE DREAM UNFOLDS	___ $5.50 U.S.	___ $6.50 CAN.
66061	THE DREAM	___ $5.50 U.S.	___ $5.99 CAN.

(limited quantities available)

TOTAL AMOUNT	$_____
POSTAGE & HANDLING	$_____
($1.00 for one book; 50¢ for each additional)	
APPLICABLE TAXES*	$_____
TOTAL PAYABLE	$_____

(check or money order—please do not send cash)

To order, complete this form and send it, along with a check or money order for the total above, payable to MIRA Books®, to: **In the U.S.:** 3010 Walden Avenue, P.O. Box 9077, Buffalo, NY 14269-9077; **In Canada:** P.O. Box 636, Fort Erie, Ontario, L2A 5X3.

Name:_____

Address:_____ City:_____

State/Prov.:_____ Zip/Postal Code:_____

Account Number (if applicable):_____

075 CSAS

*New York residents remit applicable sales taxes.
  Canadian residents remit applicable
  GST and provincial taxes.

MIRA®

Visit us at www.mirabooks.com   MBD0401BL